"I've got to watch myself around you," Paige teased. "You make it too easy for me to let my guard down."

Her softly spoken words made the decision for him.

Torrian strolled to where Paige was perched on the counter. He put his hands on either side of her, and seeing permission in her eyes, leaned in close and captured her lips in a slow, gentle kiss.

Nothing had ever tasted this good.

She was soft and sweet and more delicious than the most decadent dessert. Torrian tested his tongue against her lips, begging them to open, aching inside when they didn't. He crept along the invisible line of propriety, cautious of going too far too soon. He wouldn't take more than she was willing to give.

His arousal strained against his fly. He was dying to push Paige's tight skirt up to her waist so her legs could open for him. He was desperate to touch her. He wanted to experience the moist, hot feel of her core against his fingers.

"Aren't you going to say anything?" he asked. "Otherwise, how am I supposed to know if I'm allowed to do it again?"

"You're allowed," she answered immediately.

Books by Farrah Rochon

Kimani Romance

Huddle with Me Tonight

FARRAH ROCHON

had dreams of becoming a fashion designer as a teenager, until she discovered she would be expected to wear something other than jeans to work every day. Thankfully, the coffee shop where she writes does not have a dress code.

Farrah is an avid sports fan—when she is not penning stories, she feeds her addiction to football by attending New Orleans Saints games.

HUDDLE
with Me Tonight

FARRAH ROCHON

KIMANI™
ROMANCE

Dedicated to the memory of Andrea Taromina Pool.
My life is richer because you were a part of it.

I thank my God every time I remember you.
—*Philippians* 1:3

KIMANI PRESS™

Recycling programs
for this product may
not exist in your area.

ISBN-13: 978-0-373-86179-8

HUDDLE WITH ME TONIGHT

Copyright © 2010 by Farrah Roybiskie

www.kimanipress.com

Printed in U.S.A.

Dear Reader,

I was taught at an early age that football is more than just casual entertainment on a Sunday afternoon—it's a way of life. And when it comes to football, I'm a bona fide fanatic. This game has everything—competition and drama, and let's not forget the fine men in skintight pants. What's not to love?

It gives me great pleasure to make my Kimani Romance debut by introducing you to the yummiest men in football, the New York Sabers. This cast of hotties is as good off the field as they are on it, and are sure to please both fanatics and non-sports fans alike.

I had such fun writing *Huddle with Me Tonight*. From the action on the football field to the Iron Chef–style cooking competition, this book contains something for everyone. I hope you enjoy reading Torrian and Paige's story as much as I enjoyed writing it.

Stay tuned for upcoming stories featuring other members of the New York Sabers. I have a feeling that once you get a taste, you'll be hooked!

I love hearing from readers. E-mail me at farrah@farrahrochon.com, drop by my Web site, www.farrahrochon.com, or look me up on Facebook!

Many blessings,

Farrah Rochon

Chapter 1

"Dang, Uncle T, this place is the bomb!"

Torrian looked up from the forms and grinned at the awed look on his nephew's face as Dante and Torrian's older sister, Deirdre, walked through the front doors.

Shoving aside the florist's estimate, Torrian headed to the front of the restaurant. He greeted Deirdre with a kiss and clasped his sixteen-year-old nephew on the back.

Dante's cell phone rang. "I gotta get this," he said and left through the doors they'd just entered.

"Look at the progress they've made," Deirdre marveled.

The former warehouse had undergone major changes. Torrian had spent most of his time in the off-season shuttling between the Sabers training facility in Jersey, and overseeing the renovations of the restaurant.

They'd maintained the warehouse style and infused it with rich, warm colors. Exposed brick walls had been distressed to resemble those found in the prewar buildings that littered

Manhattan, and seventeen-foot-high ceilings were crisscrossed with dull gray air-conditioning ducts. Despite the carefully crafted rough edges, the restaurant maintained an air of elegance.

Deirdre had handpicked the kitchen equipment but had insisted Torrian have input on other aspects of the restaurant because it was his namesake and his money paying for it. He might be the venture's sole financier, but this restaurant was all for Deirdre—small repayment for everything she'd given up in her life to raise him.

The smile that now lit up Deirdre's face made every check he'd written worth it.

"I tried to imagine what it would look like, but I never could have imagined this." Deirdre shook her head as she did another slow turn. "I can't believe it's really happening."

"I told you I would do this for you, didn't I?"

Making Deirdre's dream a reality was the least he could do. Following the death of their parents, Deirdre had stepped up big time. Instead of accepting the college scholarship she'd earned, Deirdre had taken a job as a cook in a local restaurant so that Torrian—fifteen-years-old and an inch away from a life of trouble—wouldn't have to move to Atlanta with their aging great-aunt and great-uncle. The older couple would not have been able to contain the boy he'd been back then.

The day she'd asked the coach to find a spot for Torrian on the high school football team was the most pivotal day of Torrian's life. No one had known that Torrian possessed a natural athleticism that would blossom under Coach Johnson's tutelage, and lead to a scholarship and stellar football career at the University of South Carolina.

Deirdre had busted her butt, taking on a second job to pay the expenses Torrian's scholarship had not covered. She'd put her own dreams on hold. For him.

It was payback time.

While Deirdre examined the kitchen to make sure it had been arranged as she'd instructed, Torrian returned to the heap of paperwork he'd had no idea would accompany getting a restaurant off the ground. Ten minutes later, Deirdre sidled up to the table and patted him on the arm.

Torrian sent a smile over his shoulder. "Kitchen up to snuff?"

"Perfect, as is everything else." She sat across from him. "Did you meet with your publisher today?"

He nodded. "This book release is going to be awesome. The publisher is planning a mega-media blitz. They sent out advance copies to reviewers around the country, and they're putting life-sized cutouts of me in major bookstores."

"It was genius to have your memoir come out on the restaurant's opening night," Deirdre said.

"The reservation service said we're getting a hundred calls a day from people wanting to be put on the waiting list," Torrian said.

"God, I hope I can handle all of this," Deirdre sighed, nervous excitement shining in her eyes.

"It'll be a piece of cake, Dee. I know you can do this."

Dante slammed through the restaurant's doors and bounded down the steps. "Hey, Uncle T, were you able to get all ten tickets for the game?"

Torrian pulled the keys to his BMW 580i from his pocket and tossed them to his nephew. "Glove compartment."

"Now why does he need ten tickets for the game?" Deirdre asked after Dante left.

Torrian shrugged. "I guess he's bringing a few friends with him."

"Dante doesn't have ten friends," Deirdre argued. "He needs to understand that his Uncle Torrian cannot hook him up every time he wants to impress his friends."

"He's just having fun."

"He's spoiled," Deirdre complained.

"It's time someone in the family had the chance to get spoiled."

She sent him a glare.

Torrian held up his hands in surrender. "Just kidding," he chuckled. "The next time he asks for something, my answer is no. Come on." He motioned for her with his head as he flipped opened a four-inch black binder. "The decorator left samples for the tablecloths."

"What do you think of teal?" Deirdre asked, lifting a square of silky fabric. "It'll match the Sabers' team colors."

"Nah," Torrian said. "I don't want this place tied to the Sabers any more than it already is."

"Why, do you plan on getting traded anytime soon?" Deirdre laughed.

Torrian pasted on his best grin. His sister's jab hit closer to home than she could possibly know.

Actually, a trade was the least of his worries these days. Depending on the prognosis he received when he saw his private ophthalmologist in a couple of days, it was possible he wouldn't play for another NFL team ever again. He couldn't hide his eye condition from the team doctors much longer.

Anxiety instantly fisted in his gut.

He couldn't allow that to happen. Football was his life!

If he couldn't play anymore, what good was he to anyone?

I applaud Mr. Sanderson's effort to try something new and innovative with his debut novel, but there is something to be said for the tried and true. What could have been a fresh, fun take on a Shakespearean classic met a death more tragic than Macbeth's due to the author's over-the-top scenarios and tendency to over dramatize.

Next time, Mr. Sanderson, leave the real writing to the true literary geniuses.

"And send."

Paige Turner clicked the computer mouse and leaned back in her ergonomic chair. "That one is going to ruffle some feathers," she surmised as she lifted the mug of tea to her lips. She wondered how long it would take the Web site's content manager to respond to the book review she'd just posted to her blog.

This was the fourth author from this publishing house to receive an unflattering review on her book review blog, *Page Turners with Paige Turner,* the online supplement to her entertainment column in *Big Apple Weekly* magazine.

She was used to the backlash. No one liked a negative review, and now that her column was quickly becoming *the* place New Yorkers looked to when they wanted the inside scoop on what was hot in the Big Apple, they certainly didn't want a negative review from *her.*

Most authors adhered to the adage that even unflattering publicity was good publicity, requesting Paige review their new releases even though it was likely the books would get slammed. Yet others believed their work was good enough to impress her.

"Was that your motive, Mr. Smallwood?"

Paige picked up the copy of the highly anticipated combination cookbook and memoir of the star wide receiver for the New York Sabers. *In the Hot Seat: The Life and Times of Torrian Smallwood* was one of the most talked-about books of the fall.

"You *are* hot," Paige mused. The book's glossy dust jacket showcased the football player's spectacular six-pack abs and chiseled chest to full effect. The brown skin stretched taut over all those muscles reminded her of the milk chocolate silk sheets on her bed. Shadowed under the cover of his gray-and-teal Sabers helmet were breathtaking hazel eyes and a smile that alone was worth the book's retail price.

Too bad the content had not done much to impress.

Paige thumbed through the pages, which alternated between recipes and short anecdotal stories about the seven-year NFL veteran. Paige couldn't help but roll her eyes at the lame football-themed names that had been given to the recipes. Tailgating Taters. Touchdown Tomato Soup.

"Give me a break," Paige snorted.

She skimmed over one of the parts she *had* enjoyed, a retelling of how a seven-year-old Torrian had set his mother's kitchen on fire after attempting to make chicken soup for his sick Labrador retriever, earning himself the name Fire Starter. The nickname had carried over to his days of playing football. ESPN now had a special "Fire Starter Moment of the Day" when they covered a Sabers game.

Maybe she should have said something about this story instead of harping on the recipe titles?

Paige shook off the thought. Her fans would accuse her of going easy on Torrian Smallwood, and she didn't go easy on anyone, no matter who they were.

She set the book aside so she could sift through the backlog of e-mails inundating her inbox.

"Nope, don't need to refinance my house, and I definitely don't need any discount Viagra."

Paige deleted the rest of the spam, then replied to a couple of fan e-mails. She soaked in the praise. Every response on her blog or e-mail she received from a reader who agreed with her assessment sent her brain on its own private little victory dance. Her newfound success was the ultimate payback to those classmates who'd snickered when she'd been called on to read in class; the teachers who'd called her slow. Stupid.

Paige's eyelids slid shut. Her body tensed. It always did when she remembered the acute fear that held her prisoner for so many years. Sitting at her school desk, trying to make herself invisible, praying she could get through the day without anyone finding out.

And when they did. God, how she'd suffered.

The popularity of her weekly column was vindication. The girl who couldn't read was making a name for herself as a writer. It was poetic justice at its finest.

Determined to shake off the lingering queasiness she always suffered when memories of the years before her reading disorder had been diagnosed decided to bombard her, Paige sorted through more e-mails, forwarding review requests to Angela Pensky, the content manager for the magazine's Web site. She sifted through invitations to several new gallery exhibits, copying those that were feasible into her computer's calendar that linked electronically to her BlackBerry.

Already tired of e-mail, she clicked over to the comments section on her blog. In the fifteen minutes since she'd uploaded her latest book review, there had already been thirty-two responses posted. Paige grinned as she read the comments from her loyal—bordering on zealous—legion of readers, who thanked her for her honest assessment of Christopher Sanderson's book. Paige posted a response, thanking them in return for continuing to support her blog and weekly column.

An e-mail notification popped onto the screen.

ARE YOU CRAZY!!!!! was written in all caps in the subject line of an e-mail from apensky@bigappleweekly.com. The message in the body of the e-mail was a request for Paige to call her ASAP.

Just as she reached for her cell phone, it rang.

"Hello, Angie," Paige answered, recognizing the number.

"Are you crazy?" Angie screeched. "The people at Goldstein Publishing are going to go ballistic. They're tired of you trashing their books."

"Then why do they still request reviews? Better yet, why don't they find a few quality writers?"

"I'm sure they believe they *do* have quality writers. You're the one who keeps trashing them! I know the fans thrive on the criticism, but couldn't you tamper it a little?"

"I get paid to give my opinion, Angie."

"Well color your opinion," Angela said.

"Absolutely not!" She pointed to the computer screen. "Look at the responses I've gotten already. Dozens of people are thanking me for saving them $26.95."

Angie's sigh came through the phone loud and clear. "And what about your review of Torrian Smallwood's book?"

"What about it?" Paige lifted the hardback book from the desk. There may not be much substance between the pages, but the cover could be framed and mounted on the wall. The man's chest was a work of art.

"Fans of the New York Sabers should be relieved that Torrian Smallwood plays ball better than he tells a story?" Angela read directly from the review Paige had e-mailed her an hour ago.

"And?" Paige asked.

Another sigh from Angela. "You're shooting yourself in the foot with this review, you know? The grand opening for his restaurant coincides with his book's release. If you give him a good review, maybe we can score an invitation. There's still time to change it."

"As much as I would love to be surrounded by Sabers players, I'm pretty sure the reservations for opening night were scooped up the minute Torrian Smallwood announced he would be opening a restaurant. He doesn't need to bribe restaurant critics into visiting his place. Besides…" Paige paused to drain the remainder of her now lukewarm tea "…I wouldn't sell out my integrity for one of those invitations, no matter how coveted they are."

"Not even if it were at a table with Randall Robinson *and* Kendall Fisher?"

"Not even for them," Paige said. Although the thought of spending time with a heavily muscled football player did have a certain appeal. It had been a while since she'd been in the company of *any* man, let alone the likes of the fine cast of the Sabers.

"I don't believe a word out of your lying mouth," Angie laughed.

"I need to head out to the market so I can pick up the ingredients for…" Paige peered at the cookbook "…Tailback Tilapia," she finished with a snort. "These recipe names are so ridiculous."

"Yet you're trying them out?"

"I didn't say the recipes were bad, but you've got to admit the names are silly."

"Just remember that Torrian Smallwood is a huge name in this town," Angie warned before disconnecting.

After changing into a light sweater and jeans, she picked up the book and flipped through a few more pages. She jotted down the ingredients for Point-After Potato Soup, Sideline Sweet Corn Casserole, and the Field Goal French Dip Sandwich.

Paige rolled her eyes again, and knew this wouldn't be the last time. The recipe names weren't even clever, they were just plain stupid. Hopefully whoever had given the star wide receiver these recipes—Paige had no doubt that someone else had developed and tested them; she couldn't imagine the Sabers player in the kitchen—had done a better job than whoever came up with the recipe titles.

Setting her computer to hibernate mode, she tucked her list of ingredients in her purse and headed out the door.

Chapter 2

Paige rounded the corner of Mancini's Grocery and spotted the owner in his usual spot, just outside the door, a green apron tied around his waist and a broom in his hand.

"How's it going, Bruno?"

"Just fine, Ms. Turner," he answered, giving the sidewalk in front of the store's entrance a sweep, then extending his hand to help her up the single step. "Got a special treat in the store today: celebrities," Bruno said.

"Really? You finally got Jerry Seinfeld into your store?"

"Not yet." Bruno shook his head. "A couple of Sa—"

A large woman with a teased hairdo stomped out of the store. "Bruno Mancini, this artichoke is not fresh," she barked.

Paige gave Bruno an apologetic shrug as she left him to handle the irate shopper. She unfolded her canvas grocery bag and went straight for the produce section. She wasn't sure about the artichoke in question, but as far as Paige was concerned Bruno stocked the freshest produce for miles. It was one of the reasons she walked six blocks out of her way to shop here.

Paige squeezed a Roma tomato and placed it in her bag. She heard the slight commotion before she looked up and saw it reflected in the mirrored wall behind the tomato display.

Paige's eyes widened. "Oh, good God."

Torrian Smallwood and Theo Stokes. They were there. *Right* there.

And here she was, looking like a rag doll.

Torrian finished signing an autograph and left his teammate, stepping into the produce section. Paige pulled her Running Princess cap farther down until the bill nearly touched her brow. She tucked her canvas bag in close and tried to surreptitiously walk away.

No such luck.

She ran smack into a solid wall of muscle instead. Her grocery bag fell to the floor.

"Oh, excuse me," Paige said, glancing up. The sight caused an instant zing to shoot down her spine. He was twelve hundred and eighty times more gorgeous in person than he was on her tiny fifteen-inch television screen. He'd have to get rid of that shirt for her to determine if the real-life Torrian could top the picture on the cover of his book, though.

He wore a cap. Pulled low across his forehead.

"Excuse me," he said, his voice as smooth as butter.

Paige stooped to the floor to retrieve her bag. Torrian crouched beside her. "Let me help you with that."

"It's okay, I've got it."

They reached for the tomato at the same time, their fingers touching. Electricity raced through her blood, traveling like lightning to the spot where his slightly rough fingers connected with hers. He looked from their hands to her face and that same electrical current shot across the span of air between them.

Paige pulled her hand away first, but she couldn't tear her eyes from his. They slowly rose from their crouch together; their twin gazes never wavering.

"Here you go." Torrian held the tomato out to her. "Wait." He pulled it back before Paige could grab hold of it. "This one's a bit bruised." He picked another tomato from the display. "Here we are. This one's perfect."

"Um…thank you," Paige said, reaching for the tomato.

He pulled it just out of her reach and extended his right hand instead. "I'm Torrian, by the way."

"Yeah, I know," Paige answered, staring at his extended hand. Something in her brain told her not to touch it. Temptation came in so many forms, and six-plus feet of decadent chocolate male was definitely temptation at its worst.

Or best.

"I guess my attempt at going incognito has utterly failed," he said, the corner of his mouth tipping up in a smile. The effect was devastating to her good sense. Despite her brain's warning, Paige captured the hand he offered.

"I'm…." The review of his book she'd just posted jumped to the forefront of her mind. He'd find out who she was soon enough.

A different churning started in Paige's gut. One she wasn't used to. Regret.

"I'm Olivia," she said, offering her given name, which she hadn't gone by in years. Her mother was the only person who still called her Olivia.

"It's nice to meet you, Olivia," he said, finally handing her the tomato. "In fact, it may just be the best thing that's happened to me all day."

Oh yeah, he was good. Like many of his New York Sabers

teammates, Torrian Smallwood had a reputation of only having to crook his finger to bring ladies flocking to his side. He didn't have to use a finger, Paige thought. One shot of that smile was enough.

He wouldn't be smiling if he knew about her review.

"Thanks for helping," Paige said. She tried to walk past him, but he caught her elbow. Paige looked down to where he gripped her arm, then back up into his mesmerizing hazel eyes.

He let her go, as if he hadn't realized he'd been holding on to her. "Can I treat you to a cup of coffee?" he asked. "You know, to make up for running into you." That grin lit up his eyes again, and Paige knew if she didn't get away soon she would be lost.

"I'm sorry. I have to go," she said.

"Hey, Wood, you done?" Theo Stokes called.

"Almost," Torrian said. He returned his attention to Paige. "Come on, Olivia. Let me be a gentleman and buy you coffee."

Paige was a hot second from falling under the spell of that sexy voice.

"Really. I have to go," she said. Tossing the tomato back with the others, she shot out of Mancini's like a rocket.

"Boo yah!" Cedric Reeves slapped the domino on the table in Torrian's rec room with a loud smack. "Deal with that." The third-year running back leaned back in his chair, a huge grin on his face.

Torrian looked over at Theo, and they both shook their heads, matching rueful smiles tugging at their lips. The fourth member of their quartet, Jared Dawson, shot Cedric a barrage of curses that had them all laughing.

"We need to start laying some funds on these games so I can really get serious with you clowns," Cedric said.

Jared raised his hands. "Once money hits the table, I back the hell up."

"Ah, man, the league can't say anything about you betting on a friendly game of dominoes," Cedric said.

"Doesn't matter," Jared shook his head. "I'm not taking any chances."

Torrian didn't blame him. The cornerback and punt returner had nearly been kicked out of the league because of his gambling issues.

"The whole point to this is relaxing after the game. It's not about money," Torrian reminded Cedric.

Their Sunday afternoon tradition began three years ago, during Cedric's rookie season, when his tendency to speak before thinking nearly got his butt kicked by the Sabers entire offensive line. Theo had been the one to suggest they find another place to hang out after home games, away from the rest of the team. Torrian's well-equipped man cave, with its high-def flat screen, pool table and card/dominoes table, turned out to be the perfect spot.

"Can we please get back to playing dominoes," Theo suggested.

Jared went for the last slice of pizza. "Damn, Wood, I sure miss your sister cooking for us," he said, calling Torrian by the nickname most of his teammates used.

Torrian had suffered the obligatory ribbing over his last name. It had been especially brutal in the testosterone-suffused NFL locker rooms, but he never let it bother him. He'd had enough compliments from past girlfriends to offset any of the "small wood" jokes.

Cedric gestured toward the TV. "Turn it up. They're talking about today's game."

Dominoes were forgotten as all eyes focused on the seventy-two-inch LCD flat panel television mounted to the wall.

"It looks like Torrian Smallwood has shaken off the sting

of last year's devastating loss to Green Bay in the NFC Championship game," the blond sportscaster said. "His game-winning touchdown in the final seconds of today's showdown against Arizona helped to extend the team's winning streak to six and one on the season. Now, let's see if Mr. Smallwood's luck on the field will extend to his newest venture as author and restauranteur."

"Luck?" Torrian's head reared back. "Somebody needs to tell baby girl that's not luck; it's natural-born talent."

"I don't care what you call it, as long as you keep it up," Theo said from the opposite side of the table. "My finger is tired of being naked. I've got to get me a Super Bowl ring before I retire."

A fistful of popcorn went sailing past Theo's head. "Aw, man, cut that out. You're not going anywhere," Cedric said.

"I think he's bluffing, too," Torrian said. He looked over at Cedric. "You better pick up that popcorn before you leave."

"I will, Wood, damn," Cedric grumbled. He nodded toward Theo. "Straight up, Theo, you really thinking about retiring?"

"Heck, yeah," the twelve-year-veteran middle linebacker answered. "If I don't hang my shoulder pads up soon, both my knees will be shot to hell. Remember, I'm not as young as you boys. My body's been taking hits for a long time."

Torrian sat back in his chair, toying with his dominoes. He and Theo had talked about his eventual retirement, and Torrian knew the real story. Theo had his sights set on a commentator job with a new cable sports network that was starting up next year.

"What's happening on the entertainment scene, Karen?" came the news anchor's overly excited voice.

Jared nodded to the screen. "Sports is over. Change it to the San Diego/Seattle game."

Torrian grabbed the remote and was poised to flip the

channel when he heard, "Speaking of the Sabers star wide receiver, it looks like Torrian Smallwood's luck *did* run out, at least as far as his book is concerned." The news anchor's voice was saccharine sweet as she continued. "The lady with her finger on the pulse of New York's entertainment scene, Paige Turner, had a less-than-favorable review of the Sabers player's upcoming book. She found the writing elementary, and the recipes a joke. Viewers can read the rest of what Ms. Turner had to say by logging on to Big Apple Weekly dot com."

The only sound in the room was the crunch of the potato chip Cedric had just stuffed in his mouth.

Torrian turned to face his teammates. "Who the hell is Paige Turner?"

Cedric looked at him as if he were from another planet. "You don't know Paige Turner? Man, I hardly even read and I know who Paige Turner is."

"*Hardly* read?" Jared asked.

"Shut up," Cedric shot back.

"You want to stop the nonsense and tell me just who this Paige Turner is and why she's important enough for the evening news to care what she thinks about my book?"

Theo waved him off. "Don't sweat it, man. People are going to scoop up that book because of who you are, no matter what."

"I don't know, Wood." Cedric shook his head. "Paige Turner holds some power when it comes to what's happening around the city."

A couple of the popcorn kernels that had hit Theo made their way back across the table as he flung them at Cedric's head.

"Are you really going to listen to a man who probably hasn't read a book since elementary school?" Theo asked.

Cedric came back with a reply, but Torrian had tuned out

their bickering. He was more concerned with this Paige Turner person, and just how influential she was with New Yorkers.

Torrian had no doubt his book would sell. He had fans across the country. But his prime objective was making the restaurant a success for Deirdre, and he had purposely intertwined the restaurant and book. If the book garnered any negative attention, it could possibly spill over to the restaurant.

This was his sister's dream. He wasn't about to let some critic mess things up.

"I need to check out something upstairs," Torrian said, dropping his dominoes and pushing away from the table.

"Oh, come *on*, man!"

"We're in the middle of a game!"

"I'll be right back," Torrian called. "Order another pizza."

He climbed the stairs that led from his professionally decorated basement/recreation room to the main floor of the four-story brownstone he owned in New York's low-key Murray Hill neighborhood. His living space occupied the basement and first two floors. He'd had the third floor converted into a two-bedroom apartment for Deirdre and Dante, and the entire fourth floor held a state-of-the-art workout facility.

Torrian entered his office, logged on to the Internet and typed *Big Apple Weekly* into the search engine. It took him to the magazine's home page. The cover of his book was front and center. Torrian clicked on it.

"Hey, Wood, what you up to?"

Torrian turned, finding Theo just inside the door. "Nothing," he said.

"Yeah, right," Theo laughed. His teammate hitched his head toward the computer. "That's home girl? Dang, Cedric wasn't lying."

"What?" Torrian turned his attention back to the screen. And froze.

It was *her*. Olivia.

And she looked even better than she had at the grocery store he and Theo had stepped into on their way to Theo's apartment yesterday. She had light brown eyes, a short, Halle Berry-before-the-*X-Men*-movies haircut, and a smile like somebody with a secret to tell.

"That can't be her," Torrian whispered under his breath. But it was. The headshot smiling back at him was the same woman who'd occupied his mind for the past twenty-four hours. Other than today's game, he hadn't been able to concentrate on anything for longer than a few minutes before those thoughts were trampled out of his mind by images of her.

"What'd she say about the book?" Theo asked.

Torrian clicked on her picture. It opened up another page. *Page Turners with Paige Turner* ran across the top, in a flowing red script.

Hugging the left side of the screen was a full body shot of her in a self-assured pose, her arms crossed over her chest and a confident, yet soft, smile gracing her lips. Those light brown eyes were so vivid that they nearly popped off the screen. It was a big difference from the beauty in jeans and a baseball cap, though both had taken his breath away as effectively as a linebacker's shoulder to his solar plexus.

Disbelief and disappointment pummeled his chest, then was instantly replaced by the kind of resentment he'd not felt toward a woman in a long time. Who'd given Olivia…Paige… whatever her name was, the right to trash his book?

"Ah, she's got a blog," Theo said.

Torrian flashed Theo a sardonic glare. "I don't do blogs. The only thing I use the Internet for is answering fan e-mails and surfing ESPN.com."

His teammate pushed Torrian's hand away from the

computer mouse. "You need to keep up with the times, Wood. I'm thinking about starting up a blog myself." Theo scrolled down the page. Torrian caught a glimpse of his book cover.

"Hold on. Go back up."

Theo slowly scrolled up the page.

The Fire Starter's Book Leaves Me Cold, was in bold letters.

Theo started reading the paragraph under the heading out loud. "Fans of the New York Sabers should be relieved that Torrian Smallwood plays ball better than he tells a story."

"I can read," Torrian shot at him. He continued reading to himself.

Being a huge Sabers fan, I wanted to love this book, but in deference to my promise to remain honest with my readers, the most I can give Torrian Smallwood's book is two out of five coffee cups, and one of those cups is strictly for the drool factor of the wide receiver's picture on the front cover. For those who enjoy a little beefcake in the kitchen, Mr. Smallwood's book cover definitely delivers.

However, that's all it delivers. If you're expecting engaging writing, look elsewhere. While I feel for Torrian Smallwood's plight, losing his parents at the age of fifteen and being raised by his older sister, I just don't get what makes his story unique. Half the players in the National Football League defied the odds to land where they are now. Does Torrian Smallwood deserve a space on your coveted bookshelves because of his slightly interesting life? This reader doesn't think so.

As for the cookbook aspect of this "literary doubleheader," I was actually impressed with some of the recipes. When followed to the letter, there are a few very tasty dishes. Their titles, however, leave much to be desired. I can only assume the publisher's goal was to charm readers with the football-esque theme, but whoever chose the unimaginative recipe names should be bused to the very end of the creative writing chain. The recipe titles managed to land Mr. Smallwood's book in the ridiculous category.

Straightening from where he'd been leaning over Torrian's shoulder, Theo let out a low whistle. "Dawg, she chewed you up and spit you out."

Torrian sat back in his chair, torn between being hurt and being royally pissed off. He'd told his agent those recipe titles were stupid. But for her to call his life only *slightly* interesting? *That* chafed his skin like a bad rash.

"What difference does it make what she thinks about my book?" Torrian flicked a nonchalant wave at the screen. Although, to him, it *did* matter.

"Looks like it makes a difference to some people out there. There's already a hundred sixty-eight responses."

Torrian clicked where Theo pointed. Theo read the first three responses out loud, which all echoed the same thought: The review wouldn't affect their decision to buy the book or eat at the Fire Starter Grille as soon as they were able to get a reservation. Torrian felt vindicated. He knew his fans wouldn't let some book critic influence them.

"Told you," Theo said. "For some crazy reason, people just like you."

Torrian went back with his elbow, playfully catching his teammate in the gut. Torrian had to admit her review had affected him. Everything about her had.

A thought occurred to him, nearly knocking Torrian out of his chair. This review must be why she'd turned down his invitation for coffee. She knew she'd just ripped his book to shreds and posted it for the entire world to see. He hadn't just imagined that spark that had ignited between them.

But did it even matter now? Looking back at the computer screen and the words Olivia—Paige, he reminded himself—had written about him, the spark had undeniably fizzled. Yet he couldn't deny it was still there, smoldering like embers just waiting to catch fire. From the moment his eyes had connected with hers, Torrian had been seized by the instant attraction that had arced between them.

The doorbell rang.

"Probably the pizza," Theo said. "Forget about this, Wood. We need to finish up the domino game. I'm meeting Latoya for dinner tonight, and I want to chill out at the crib before heading back out again."

"She remembers I'm coming to see her later this week?" Torrian lowered his voice, even though the only other people in the house were still downstairs in the basement. Theo's sister, Latoya Stokes, MD, was his personal ophthalmologist, and the soul of discretion, thank goodness.

"Yeah, she knows," Theo said.

Satisfied after reading the first few responses to Paige Turner's bogus review, Torrian shut down the Internet and followed Theo out of his office. He refused to even acknowledge the hurt that continued to tug at his chest.

He wouldn't think about an insignificant chance encounter in the produce section when he thought of Paige Turner. She couldn't be that woman to him. She was the woman who'd trashed him and publicized it to the world.

That's what he would remember when he thought of Paige Turner.

Chapter 3

"Tell Dante I have that jersey he asked for," Torrian said to his sister. He grinned as Deirdre went on another tirade about Dante being spoiled.

Hanging up the phone, he skimmed e-mails, answering a few but ignoring the haters who always found something to criticize, even after he had stellar games like the one he'd had today. His dropped pass in the third quarter only fueled their criticism, even though he'd made up for it with two fourth-quarter touchdowns.

He told himself not to do it, yet Torrian found himself typing the Web address for *Big Apple Weekly*. He clicked on the link to Paige Turner's blog.

It was up to 347 comments.

"Damn, it's only been a few hours."

He skimmed over the comments he'd read earlier, smiling at the way his fans stuck up for him. As he scrolled down the page, Torrian's smile, along with his stomach, started to drop.

More and more people were agreeing with Paige, saying that pro athletes should stick to what they do best. One fan posted that she thought it was a joke that Torrian Smallwood would try to put out a book. That it was an even bigger joke that he would try opening a restaurant.

Torrian's stomach bottomed out.

No. *No.*

Talking about him or his book was one thing; bringing the Fire Starter Grille into the mix was an entirely different matter. There was too much riding on the restaurant's performance— the realization of his sister's lifelong dream.

And now, because of one woman's opinion, hundreds of New Yorkers were starting to doubt its appeal.

Without thinking, Torrian clicked on the Add a Comment button and fired off a response to Paige Turner. He hit the submit button and sat back with a satisfied sigh.

Then his common sense kicked in.

"What in the hell did I just do?"

He searched frantically for a way to retract his response, his entire body sagging in relief when he saw the message in italics under his comment stating that he had five minutes to edit or delete his response before it would be permanently archived.

"Guess they put that in for stupid hotheads who react before they think," Torrian murmured. He scrolled over the Edit button.

"Uncle T! Help!"

Torrian's heart stopped at his nephew's yelp. He hopped up from behind his desk and ran out of his office. Dante came charging around the corner.

"What's going on?"

"Your sister. She's gone crazy!" Dante ran past Torrian and slammed the office door closed.

Deirdre came stomping through the front door.

"Where is he?" she growled. She was dressed in a cotton bathrobe, her hair tied under a silk scarf, house slippers on her feet. For a second, Torrian was catapulted back to his teenage days. How many times had Deirdre been standing at the front door of their old house dressed the same way, waiting for him to come in after missing curfew?

"Keep her away from me," Dante said through the door.

His sister plopped one hand on a thick hip and wagged a tennis shoe at Torrian with the other. "This is his fourth time missing curfew this month. He wasn't supposed to be out in the first place. He's on punishment."

"Tell her I'm a man, Uncle T. She can't be putting me on punishment."

"Don't get in the middle of this," Deirdre warned.

"Get in the middle, Uncle T!" came the call from beyond the door.

Torrian laughed as he wrung the shoe from Deirdre's hand. "Get out here, Dante," he shouted at the door. "If you're a man, then come out and face your Mom like one."

His nephew poked his head out the crack he'd made in the door. "She put that shoe away?"

Torrian raised the tennis shoe. "She's unarmed."

Dante reluctantly came out of the office but stayed close to the door.

"Now, want to explain why you left the house when you were on punishment?" Torrian asked.

"Because I shouldn't be on punishment," was Dante's dumb answer.

"That's not your call to make," Torrian replied.

Dante opened his mouth but shut it without saying a word. At least his nephew had caught a clue. On his way out the front door, Dante picked up the jersey from the foyer table.

Torrian heard Deirdre clear her throat. He looked over

at her, took in her rigidly set jaw and the stern warning in her eyes.

"Uh, sorry, Dawg, but I'm gonna have to take the jersey back. I can't let you have it after sneaking out."

Dante looked from Torrian to his mother, his face mottled with anger. He left the apartment in full-pout mode, showing just how much of a little boy he still was. Torrian turned to Deirdre and hunched a shoulder. "He's sixteen."

"I don't know what I'm going to do with him. He defies me at every turn."

"That's what boys do at that age. Remember me at sixteen?"

Deirdre shook her head. "You were never like this." She bit her lower lip and looked away. When she turned, that lower lip was quivering. "I'm thinking of sending him to his father," she said. "I just can't handle him anymore."

"You don't have to do it alone. We're a team," he reminded her. "I'll talk to Dante." Torrian brought her in for another hug and kissed the top of the purple silk scarf covering her head. "Get some sleep," he said. "You've got a tough week ahead of you."

"You, too," Deirdre said. "And Torrian," she called, halting at the open door. "I heard about the book review. Don't pay any attention to Paige Turner."

Damn! He'd forgotten about the blog.

Torrian slammed the door shut behind Deirdre and raced to his computer.

The italic message stating he could edit his post was gone, and his stupid, knee-jerk response had just been posted for electronic posterity.

"Damn," Torrian whispered.

He lowered himself into the desk chair and rested his head against the soft leather. "Stupid, stupid, stupid."

His cell phone rang.

"Why would you post a comment on Paige Turner's blog?" Theo asked before Torrian could speak. "Especially one asking the woman if she even knows how to read?"

Torrian ran a hand down his face. "I didn't say that, did I?"

"Basically, yeah," Theo answered.

"I was supposed to erase it, but I got distracted," Torrian explained. "What are you doing reading her blog anyway?"

"Same reason you were reading it. I wanted to see what people were saying."

"I don't know what I was thinking," Torrian murmured, reading over his comment and wincing even more at the offensive words he'd used. He would never talk to a woman this way in person. What made him think it was okay to say it over the Internet? "I feel like a jackass," Torrian admitted.

"Yeah, well, that comment you posted there makes you look like one, too."

Torrian sat up in the chair. "It's not really permanent, is it?" His eyes roamed the Web page. "There's got to be some nerdy tech guy who can go in and erase it."

"I don't know," Theo said. "Maybe you can contact *Big Apple Weekly*. Or just e-mail Paige Turner."

"Yeah, she would just jump at the chance to erase my comment so I don't look like some bitter jerk who can't take a little criticism," Torrian snorted.

"She's a professional. She isn't going to hold a grudge."

Torrian wasn't so sure. If the shoe was on the other foot, and she had posted some ugly comment about him, he would have told her to step off. But then again, he could be a jerk. Maybe Paige Turner would be more forgiving.

He clicked the E-mail Paige button and a blank e-mail popped up with pturner@bigappleweekly.com already in the recipient window.

Torrian let out a deep breath. "Look, man, I'll talk to you

later." He disconnected from Theo and stared at the computer screen, cursing Dante for storming into the house before he had a chance to erase that stupid comment. Cursing himself for writing it in the first place.

Tail firmly between his legs, Torrian started his e-mail to Paige Turner.

Paige propped an elbow on the edge of Angela's desk and flipped through the bride magazine spread out before her. At least a half dozen just like it were stacked atop the Web content manager's desk.

As she flipped through the magazine, the serene smiles of the models in their wedding gowns reminded Paige of what had been missing from her life for far too long. She'd immersed herself in work after things had ended with Michael Weston, her last real boyfriend. But that had been two years ago! It felt like an eternity. She missed having someone to hold her at night.

An image of compelling hazel eyes and a delicious grin flashed through her brain. After the way she'd trashed the man's book, Paige doubted she'd ever be on the receiving end of a sexy grin from him again.

"What about this one?" Paige pointed to a slim, fish-tailed designer gown with a plunging neckline and beaded trim.

Angela glanced at the magazine. "I don't have big enough breasts to hold up that gown."

"Hmm, you're right," Paige agreed, and flipped the page.

Angela sent her a mean look. "Bryce happens to be a leg man," she said.

After a few seconds of trying to hold it in, Paige burst out laughing. Angela was five feet if she was an inch tall, and that was being generous.

"Fine, it's my personality," Angela said.

"Now that I'd believe."

"Uh-oh." Angela pointed at the screen. "Looks like you got under somebody's skin with that little review of yours."

Paige scooted her chair over so she could share the space in front of the computer with Angela. Posted under the name Torrian Smallwood was a response to her review of his book that left little of his feelings to the imagination.

All I see here is yet another person trying to gain their fifteen minutes of fame by blasting someone who is a thousand times more popular than they are. Can you even read, Paige Turner? If you could, then you would plainly see that the stories of my childhood are meant to be funny. It's a cookbook and autobiography, not a candidate for the Nobel Prize in Literature. Lighten up.

"Ouch." Paige forced herself to laugh, despite the sickening feeling swarming in her gut. The jab about her ability to read hit a little too close to home. And for some reason it hurt even more coming from Torrian. What happened to the charming guy who'd rescued her tomato in the produce section at Mancini's?

"Do you think it's really him?" Paige asked.

"New Yorkers are pretty bold, but I don't know if anyone has the guts to impersonate Torrian Smallwood. I told you it was a risky review before you posted it," Angela reminded her. "The man is a god in this city."

"Maybe on the football field, but that godliness doesn't transfer to his writing. He's putting out a mediocre book, so he received a mediocre review."

"He probably didn't write a word of that book," Angela surmised.

"I doubt he did," Paige agreed. "But he's allowed it to be published under his name. Therefore, *he* got the bad review."

"Was the book that dreadful? I haven't had a chance to read it."

Paige sat back in the chair and let out a sigh. "The memoir portion lacked originality to me. The writing was shoddy." She shrugged.

"And the recipes?"

"Okay, honestly, the few recipes I tried came out pretty good."

"So what was the problem?"

"The names he gave the recipes were hokey."

"Again, probably was not Torrian Smallwood to make that decision," Angela said.

"Again, his name is on it." Paige emphasized her rejoinder with a flick of the pen she was holding.

Angela conceded, giving Paige a nod and sitting back at her desk. "Well, the question now is, are you going to respond to him?"

Paige leveled her with a sardonic lift of her eyebrows. "Uh, excuse me, but did you not read the part where that man questioned my ability to read?"

Angela held up her hands as she pushed away from the desk. "I don't want to get burned by the sparks."

"There will be no sparks," Paige informed her. "For one thing, I refuse to sink to his level. But you're right; I don't want to run the risk of alienating any of his die-hard fans. I have my own following, but I'm not delusional enough to think it's even close to the Sabers fanatics in this town."

"I don't envy you here, Paige. Coming out negatively against someone as popular as Torrian Smallwood can blow up in your face, but I know it won't stop you," Angie said. She opened a desk drawer and withdrew her purse. "I'll get us some coffee while you give him a piece of your mind."

"Make mine a double shot," Paige called. She held her fingers poised over the keyboard, trying to think of a tactful, yet stern, reply to Torrian's comment.

"Let's see," she said, her bottom lip between her teeth.

Even as Paige concocted a response, a part of her let out a mournful cry.

She hadn't left Mancini's with illusions of falling into Torrian's arms and living happily ever after, but it wasn't totally out of the realm of possibility. Maybe if their paths had crossed at another time; if they had encountered each other under different circumstances. Just maybe…

But that wasn't the case. Her acquaintance with Torrian was professional. Period. She'd had to make tough choices for the sake of her career before. She couldn't allow fantasies of happily ever after to derail her from reaching her goals.

Still, she didn't want to be Torrian's enemy.

His reaction didn't surprise her. At this point in her career, she was used to hostile authors. But she'd never shared a…a *something* with those other authors. However small that something was, it had been there with Torrian. She'd felt it.

Paige took a deep breath and steeled herself against the warring emotions rioting within her brain. Her professional integrity was on the line, and it was everything to her. She wasn't about to lose credibility with her readers by recanting her review, especially since she meant every word.

"You done?" Angela came back into the office with two skinny vanilla lattes, a Monday morning ritual.

"I am," Paige said. "And I, unlike Mr. Smallwood, was very professional." She accepted the paper cup from Angela, removed the plastic cover and blew at the foam topping the cup of steaming milk and coffee. "Of course, I had to take a few gibes," Paige added. "The man did, after all, question my ability to read."

Angela paused with her cup halfway to her mouth. "What kind of gibes did you take?" she asked, her voice full of caution.

Paige twirled around in the swivel chair, "Nothing too bad. I just asked if his book writing has possibly gotten in the way of his game on the field. And suggested that if he were more focused on playing ball instead of opening a restaurant, maybe the Sabers would have made it to the Super Bowl last year."

Angela choked on the coffee she'd just sipped. "Are you suicidal? Do you know the kind of heat you're going to take for bringing up last year's NFC Championship game?"

"He intimated that I don't know how to read," Paige repeated. "Excuse me for taking offense, but because I make a living reading and writing, I'm not inclined to show Torrian Smallwood mercy."

Angela shook her head. "I don't know about this. I think you're playing with fire."

Paige eyed her coworker over the rim of her coffee cup. "Don't worry about me. I can handle the heat."

"At the risk of sounding cliché, be careful what you ask for," Angela warned. "You just might get it."

Chapter 4

Torrian hissed through his teeth. His arms quivered under the strain of the weight bar. He should have stopped twenty minutes ago, but each time he attempted to place the metal bar back into its resting place, he thought about the team doctor waiting for him just down the hall. He knew he should man up and face the music, but he wasn't ready to hear the words. He couldn't stomach the doctor telling him he could no longer play ball because of his eyes.

Guilt lodged in his throat. The internal debate had been a constant companion; his questioning of his worth to the team. In his heart, Torrian knew he was on the verge of becoming more of a liability than an asset.

Memories of last year's conference championship game ran through his mind. He'd been so close. Moving at lightning speed toward the end zone. Passed the thirty-yard line. The twenty-five. The twenty.

The hit had come out of nowhere.

Torrian's gut clinched as he recalled the force of three hundred pounds of determined linebacker plowing into him. Because of his deteriorating vision he hadn't seen the guy approaching.

He could still hear the raucous cheers of the crowd resonating through his brain. They'd had reason to cheer. Their team was headed to the Super Bowl, while his teammates were headed home.

How much longer could he stand to do this to them? How deep did his selfishness run?

The self-disgust burned a hole in his gut, but Torrian knew he wasn't ready to give up his career just yet. What was he, if not a ballplayer? He'd been nothing before football. He'd be nothing without it. He couldn't give it up. The hiding, the lying, the guilt—they would have to continue.

He clenched his eyes shut and pushed the bar up from his chest. The weight suddenly eased. He opened his eyes to find Theo directly above, both hands wrapped around the bar.

"You can stop stalling," Theo said as he lifted the bar and settled it on its holder. "Doc got called away."

Relief washed over Torrian. He prayed it didn't show on his face. "What's that got to do with anything?" he asked, sitting up and wiping sweat from his brow.

"Cut the crap, Wood," Theo said. "You know you're scared as hell something showed up on the mid-season physical. Don't worry about it. If they found anything serious, they would have called you in."

Torrian rested his elbows on his thighs and hung his head so low his chin touched his chest. "I hate this."

"I know," his teammate said, understanding saturating his words. "Just remember it's not the end of the world," Theo reminded him. "Nobody plays this game forever."

"A part of me knows that," Torrian said. "But the other part doesn't want to give up playing ball. This game is my life."

"That's bull. You've got a family. *They* are your life."

"You're right." Torrian sighed. "My main concern is taking care of Deirdre and Dante." He cut his eyes at Theo. "I hate when you start making sense."

Theo returned his grin, then asked, "Speaking of your sister, is she seeing anyone?"

Torrian's head whipped around. "What?"

"You heard me," Theo said. He raised his arms up and hooked them around the weight machine's handlebars.

"How long have you been checking out my sister?"

"Long enough," Theo said. "Why do you sound so shocked?"

"You gotta admit Deirdre's not the type of woman you usually have on your arm."

"What's that supposed to mean?" Theo asked with an affronted growl.

"Don't try to play me. Your typical woman is five-nine, a hundred pounds, and twenty-three years old, everything Deirdre is not."

"Stop making me sound so shallow, Wood. Besides, I'm getting tired of my typical woman. I'd rather spend time with someone who can hold a conversation that doesn't pertain to shopping or watching *America's Next Top Model*."

"Dee's got a lot on her plate these days, but what can I say?" Torrian shrugged. "Go for it, man. But I'm warning you, if you hurt her, I'm coming after your ass."

"I won't hurt her. I just want to get to know her better."

Cedric Reeves came into the weight room, one towel slung around his shoulders and another riding low on his hips.

"Hey, Wood, you pissed Paige Turner off something fierce, man. Did you read her latest response on the blog?"

Torrian's chest tightened. "Don't tell me she posted again."

"Oh yeah, and it ain't pretty." Cedric grinned as he headed toward the showers.

Torrian groaned and fell back on the weight bench, covering his face with his hands. He didn't know what else to do. He'd e-mailed three times since Sunday, damn near begging Paige to cut out this tit-for-tat thing they had going on her blog, but she'd ignored every one of them, choosing to keep everything out in the open.

Torrian had considered being the bigger man and apologizing, but this fight had become personal. After reading some of her past reviews, Torrian noticed a pattern. Paige Turner had it out for the rich. She occasionally had a kind word for an upcoming Broadway star's performance, or a mom-and-pop deli trying to keep its head above water in New York's saturated restaurant industry, but the positive reviews were few and far between, and virtually nonexistent for celebrity types.

He dragged his hands over his head and down his face. "I don't know what else to do," he admitted. "I've sent e-mails."

"Apologize on the blog, maybe?" Theo suggested.

"Hell, no." Torrian shook his head. He jumped up from the workbench and headed for his locker. Forget the showers. He could do that when he got home, after he took care of this latest post from her.

"You really should think about apologizing," Theo said. "You *are* the one who started it with that stupid response. You should have just left it alone."

He dropped the towel from his waist and pulled on a pair of sweats. "She started it by posting the review in the first place."

"That's her job!"

"Well, she needs to get a real job instead of giving opinions on something she knows nothing about," Torrian retorted, stuffing his arms through the sleeves of his shirt and jerking it over his head. "I'll bet she's never even tried to write a book."

"Dawg, you didn't write this book either," Theo reminded him. "You need to come with something better than that."

Torrian started to speak, then stopped. "Shut up, man," he finally said. "All this could have ended Sunday night if she'd erased that response like I asked in my e-mail. She's the one dragging this on."

It was hard to believe she was the same woman he'd met in the grocery store a week ago.

"So, what you gonna do?"

"Fight fire with fire," Torrian said. He slung his gym bag over his shoulder. "They don't call me the Fire Starter for nothing."

Angela and Paige stood at the corner of 32nd and 3rd as lunch-hour traffic whizzed toward the East River.

"So, what's the latest in the Torrian Smallwood drama?"

Paige groaned. "Don't ask."

"Uh-oh." Angie laughed. "What happened this time?"

"That man is an ass," Paige said. "Can you believe he had the nerve to come to my own blog and ask me if I started reviewing books because I was too insecure to write my own? I wanted to smack him through the computer."

"Hmm, now that I think about it, that *is* a legitimate question."

"Angie!" Paige screeched. The light changed, and the sea of bodies that had accumulated at the edge of the block flowed across the street. "I'm a columnist. I dabbled in creative writing in college, but I've never had any real aspirations to write novels. I love to eat and read and experience life, and I am lucky enough to have a job that allows me to do all of those things. Torrian Smallwood is an insecure jackass who is too stupid to recognize when he's lost the battle."

"So, are you just going to keep this up?" Angie asked. "It's been great for the Web site. This city is absolutely obsessed with the two of you."

"The publicity was cool in the beginning, but this has gotten out of hand." She looked pointedly at Angela. "But I'm not backing down first."

If she looked deep enough, Paige could admit that keeping up this online quarrel with Torrian was retaliation for him not living up to the charismatic man she'd built him up to be in her own mind. The rational part of her brain knew it wasn't fair to judge him based on a five-minute chance encounter, but the attraction had been too strong. She wanted him to be the man she'd met last weekend. Clearly, he was not.

She opened the door to the deli a block away from *Big Apple Weekly*'s offices. The owner, who knew them by name, greeted them as they walked up to the counter. Paige ordered a cup of vegetable soup and a turkey sandwich on whole-grain bread. She tried not to cringe as Angela ordered corned beef on rye with a side of coleslaw.

As soon as they sat at a table, Paige's cell phone rang. She grabbed it from her purse and saw a number she didn't recognize on the screen.

"Probably a wrong number," she said, and put the phone back into her purse without answering it. Not a minute later, the phone rang again. It was the same number.

"Just answer it," Angela said. "They're going to keep calling until you tell them they have the wrong number."

"You're right," Paige said. She answered the phone. "Hello."

There was a slight pause, then, "Is this Olivia Paige Turner?"

Paige's stomach pitched and rolled. She instantly recognized that deep voice.

"Who is it?" Angela asked before taking a huge bite of her sandwich.

Paige shushed her, then spoke into the phone. "Yes, Mr. Smallwood, it is. And I go by Paige, not Olivia."

Angela's eyes bugged. She started choking.

Paige rolled her eyes.

"I guess you know why I'm calling," Torrian said.

"I have an idea," Paige answered. "What I don't know is how you managed to get hold of my personal cell number."

"I called in a favor," he answered. Paige was inclined to believe him. She knew how things worked with these professional athletes. They were treated like royalty. Torrian Smallwood probably had people indebted to him all over this city.

"And why would you waste one of your precious favors on obtaining my phone number when you have no problem contacting me through my blog?"

"I think enough has been said on your blog," he replied.

Angela was waving at her like a maniac on crack. Paige waved her off.

"I don't know," Paige answered. "You haven't called my mother names yet. That's usually the next step in the little junior high game you're playing."

"I don't want to play any games with you, Paige." The sound of his deep voice saying her name traveled down her spine like warm honey. "I just want you to delete that stuff on your Web site, so this can all go away. It's gone too far."

"I don't recant my reviews," she said "And, to be fair, you're the one who started this little war."

"Just what did you expect after tearing my book apart the way you did?" His voice had lost a bit of its hostility. He sounded genuinely disappointed.

"I'm sorry you did not agree with my review, but I have to be honest," Paige said. "The book was weakly written. In my opinion, it lacked depth."

"Fine," came his exasperated sigh. "You're entitled to your opinion, and maybe I shouldn't have said some of the things I said on your blog. But can we please just end this? In fact, why don't you let me take you to dinner to make up for the way I've acted?"

His dinner invitation took her by surprise. If she went to dinner with him, all of New York would think the cutthroat Paige Turner had fallen under Torrian Smallwood's spell. Though God knows she was close to falling.

'I can't," Paige answer, her good sense warring with her heart. There was nothing she wanted to do more than accept his invitation to dinner.

"Come on, Paige. It's just dinner."

"I'm sorry," she said, ending the call.

With a deadpan look on her face, Angela said, "Well, that went well."

Chapter 5

"That went well," Torrian snorted.

He'd promised four tickets to this weekend's game against Denver in return for Paige's cell phone number, and had blown the call, big time.

This entire situation was driving him crazy. But what had him even more frustrated than Paige's insistence that their little online squabble remain public was his undeniable attraction to her. After the shots she'd taken at him on her blog, Paige was the *last* woman he should be attracted to, but he couldn't stop thinking about her.

After a mental journey through his past relationships, Torrian had zeroed in on the one thing that made Paige so different from all those other women.

Honesty.

So many of the women he'd dated had tried to make themselves into what they thought *he* wanted them to be, or what society thought the girlfriend of an NFL player should be. Torrian had never gotten to know who they truly were. Paige Turner was different. His celebrity didn't stop her from telling him exactly what was on her mind. It was definitely a turn-on.

He pulled into the underground garage below the North Manhattan Medical Family building where Latoya Stokes practiced. He got out of the car and walked over to Theo's Lexus LX that had pulled into a slot two spots down from him.

Theo was still on the phone as he climbed out of the luxury SUV. He laughed at whatever was said on the other line. "That's why I pay you fifteen percent. I'll catch you later." He nodded at Torrian. "How'd it go, Dawg?" Theo asked, pocketing his phone.

"Let's just say I hope your call went better than mine," he said as they headed for the elevator.

"Unless Paige Turner offered to strip naked for you, I'd say I had the better call."

Torrian reached over and slapped palms with Theo, bringing him in for a one-arm hug. "The network made an offer for the anchor position?"

"Two million a year."

"That's even more than I'd expected."

"My agent asked for three, but we knew that was a pie-in-the-sky number. We were ready to settle at one point five mil."

"You're really going to retire?"

Theo shook his head. "I don't know, Wood. It's tempting as hell. No more training camp. No more getting pounded on the field. It's hard to pass up."

"I didn't think you were serious," Torrian admitted. "But you know I'm behind you one hundred percent."

If only his call could have gone a tenth as well as Theo's, Torrian would be satisfied. The longer his responses to Paige

Turner remained on that blog, the more he looked like a jerk who had verbally attacked a woman—not just any woman, but New York's entertainment guru. As far as his image was concerned he may as well have slapped her across the face.

The elevator dinged their arrival to the fifth floor. Torrian's first visit to this office had been two years ago, when he'd first noticed that he couldn't see as far out of the corner of his left eye. He'd immediately thought of his grandfather who'd eventually gone blind because of some eye disease.

Torrian had been scared out of his mind. When he finally confessed to Theo, his teammate had made an appointment with his sister. Torrian had been ready to kill him. His biggest fear, even more than the gradually darkening spots, was the idea of the Sabers' medical staff finding out about the trouble with his vision. He was a wide receiver; hand/eye coordination was the most important aspect of his job. News of his deteriorating vision was equivalent to throwing a contract renewal into a bonfire.

But Theo promised that Latoya would be discreet. And she had been. Torrian had been to Latoya's office over a dozen times over the past two years, and they had managed to keep his condition off the front page of the *New York Post*.

"Hi, there, honey," Latoya greeted, walking straight to Torrian and enveloping him in a hug. Her short, natural locks were bound by a red, yellow and white headband that hugged her hairline. "What's with the face?" she asked.

"He just got off the phone with Paige Turner," Theo provided.

"Ah." Latoya nodded. "How'd that work out for you?"

"I had good intentions." Torrian shrugged a shoulder.

"Just bad execution?"

"Horrible execution," Torrian agreed. "She hung up in my face."

"Ouch." Latoya laughed. "Let's get started. We won't have this place to ourselves for very long."

For two years Latoya had scheduled his appointments around her partner's off days and the receptionist's lunch hour. There wasn't enough money in the world to pay back his gratitude for her unwavering dedication and discretion.

Theo's cell phone started blasting old-school Snoop Dogg. "It's my agent," he said. "I'll take this outside." He pointed to Torrian. "Try not to piss Paige Turner off while I'm away."

Latoya guided Torrian to a massive piece of machinery and he fitted his chin in the concaved chin rest.

"Tilt your head down just a bit." She flicked a switch, and the machine started to hum. "Now, look at the black dot. What did you do to get on Paige Turner's bad side?"

"I had the audacity to write a book," he snorted.

"She can be brutal when she doesn't like something. I read her weekly column every now and then. I think she's cute."

"I would have thought you had better taste," Torrian said.

"Oh, please. Don't even try it. You know she's gorgeous. Unfortunately for me, I believe she's straight."

"I don't care how she looks," Torrian lied through his teeth. He'd been thinking about how she looked from the moment he first saw her. "The woman trashed my book. And for the past week she's been attacking me on her blog."

"Theo said you attacked first."

Torrian popped up. "The hell I did."

"Put your chin back in that cradle," Latoya admonished.

Torrian settled back into his seat and leaned forward. "I especially need New York readers to be behind the book, since they're the ones who will support the restaurant," Torrian continued. "What I *don't* need is this negative publicity from Paige Turner."

"It's not necessarily negative publicity. I've bought books

she's been heavily critical of just to see if they were really as bad as she thought they were. She's usually right," Latoya tacked on.

"Thanks a lot," Torrian snorted.

"I'm sure your book is an exception." She laughed. The machine let out several beeps. "Okay, we're done."

"How much worse is it?" Torrian sighed.

"Just a little," she confirmed. She took a deep breath, and Torrian's own breath clogged in his throat. "What has me concerned is that we've seen deterioration over your last three visits. Although it is extremely slight, the fact that there is a steady decline isn't the best news."

"How much longer until I'm completely blind?" Torrian asked, knowing he wouldn't get a straight answer. It's not as if it mattered anyway. He would be kicked out of the league long before he reached the state of legal blindness.

"You know I can't answer that question," Latoya said. "Retinitis pigmentosa develops differently in different people. It's not as bad as you're probably thinking, Torrian. At the rate the disease is progressing, you still have many years of very good sight ahead of you."

"Won't matter to the NFL," he said.

Latoya patted his shoulder. "I know, honey."

Torrian covered the hand she held on his shoulder. It was too bad Latoya was gay. They got along better than he ever had with any of the women he'd dated over the years.

Theo burst through the door. "You finished?" he asked Torrian.

"Yeah, we're done," Latoya said. "I'll see you back here in another couple of months. Good luck in the game this weekend."

"Thanks, babe." Torrian kissed her goodbye and followed Theo out of the office.

"Okay, what's up?" Torrian asked as they headed up the corridor.

Theo pressed the button for the elevator. "The Sabers just made a counteroffer."

Torrian's eyebrows shot up. "Seriously?" The elevator's door opened and they stepped in.

"Yep," Theo said once the doors shut. "One year, seven million."

Torrian nearly swallowed his tongue. "Is that even an option? You playing another year?"

The elevator door opened. "I don't know, man. That's a lot of money." Theo shrugged. "Of course, I've already got a lot of money."

"It's a tough decision, Theo. You gotta figure this one out on your own. Good luck."

"You, too, Dawg. Hope you can get this thing with Paige Turner squared away."

"I'm working on it," Torrian said.

Torrian knew there was only one way to put this mess with Paige Turner to rest. He had to talk to her face to face.

His mind made up, he skimmed through the numbers in his phone's directory until he found the one he needed. Then he called in another favor.

"What do you think this injury will mean for the rest of the Sabers team?"

Torrian ran the towel over his face again before slinging it around his neck. He shifted on the bench in front of his locker, making sure the towel covering his groin didn't flap open. It was too much to ask to get dressed before the reporters barged into the locker room for their post-game interviews.

"The Sabers will be just fine," Torrian answered. "Losing one wide receiver for a few games won't hurt."

"Even if that wide receiver is the great Torrian Smallwood?" a nasally voice drawled.

Torrian ignored Barry Stein's sarcastic nonquestion. The reporter wasn't looking for an answer. He was much more concerned with getting under Torrian's skin. It had been that way since the day the sports writer had accused him of reneging on an exclusive Torrian had never promised him in the first place.

"Melanie?" Torrian pointed to the lone female reporter from the New Jersey ABC affiliate.

"Do you think the injury will require surgery?" Melanie Thomlison asked.

"Johnson's hit wasn't as bad as it looked. I mean, really, do you think that little guy can do that much damage?" He paused for the flurry of chuckles. "The only reason doc wants me to sit out is so I can rest up before the playoffs. The team is in solid position for the NFC North's top spot. There's no need to risk me getting further injured."

Torrian fielded a few more questions, many of which were just a restatement of the questions he'd already answered. Just as he was about to excuse himself, Barry Stein asked, "What do you have to say about your attack on Paige Turner?"

The rest of the reporters turned to Torrian with eyes wide and gleaming, as if they'd been wanting to ask about the Paige Turner situation but hadn't had the balls. Of course, that bastard Stein wouldn't shy away from it.

Torrian summoned his most charming smile. "If I can face what all of you throw at me without losing my cool, why on Earth would I attack an Internet blogger for a few innocent statements?" Torrian answered.

"I think Ms. Turner would resent you calling her a mere Internet blogger. She's a respected columnist and one of the most influential and *opinionated* people in New York's entertainment world."

"I don't mean to downplay Ms. Turner's influence," he backtracked. "I just want to make it clear that I have not attacked her."

"I doubt she would agree with your assessment," Stein retorted.

Torrian tried to keep the irritation from showing on his face. "This entire thing has been blown out of proportion. Paige Turner didn't enjoy my book. She has a right to her opinion. Case closed." Torrian turned toward his locker.

"If that's the case, why did you get so upset? Is it because deep down there's some truth to some of the things Paige Turner has accused you of?"

Torrian turned around. "What has she accused me of? Not knowing how to cook? If Paige Turner has any doubts about my cooking ability, I'd be happy to show her. Point me to any kitchen and I'll meet her there, then we can see who knows their way around a stove and who's just talk. That's all I'm saying about this. Now get the hell out of my locker room."

As soon as he said it, Torrian knew he'd played directly into Stein's hands. The reporter wanted him to go off half-cocked, and like an ass, that's exactly what he'd done. When would he ever learn?

Disgusted with himself, he took off for the showers. Maybe the hot water pounding down on his head would knock some sense into it.

Chapter 6

Paige closed the book and emitted a satisfied sigh. It was a rare occasion that she got the chance to read for pleasure, but after the week she'd had, she figured she deserved to indulge in a little escapism. She laid the paperback atop the book she *should* have been reading, an autobiography of a New York businessman whom many pundits believed would enter the next mayoral race. She popped the last grape into her mouth and went into the kitchen to refill her bowl, then carried it to her computer.

Paige pulled up the page for her blog and grimaced. They were up to eighteen hundred replies, by far the most her blog had ever received. She had to bury this fiasco with Torrian Smallwood. Despite the traffic to her blog, the guilt of profiting from someone else's misery wreaked havoc on her conscience. Even if that person had brought that misery upon himself.

That wasn't completely fair. Could she fault him for retaliating after the review she'd posted? Other authors had done so. Why should Torrian be held to a different standard?

Maybe because no other author's response had affected her as much as his had.

Her intercom buzzed.

Paige popped a couple of grapes into her mouth and walked over to the panel next to the door. She pressed the intercom button and spoke into the speaker. "Who is it?" she garbled.

"Torrian Smallwood."

Paige nearly choked on the grapes.

"Oh, my God," she breathed. First her cell number, and now he'd found out where she lived. An excited tingle fluttered in her chest.

"Stop it, Paige. This is stalking." She wouldn't feel this shimmer up her spine if the average Joe had found out where she lived. But Torrian was no average Joe.

The intercom buzzed again, long and steady.

"What can I do for you?" she spoke into the speaker.

"You can let me up," he suggested.

Paige disregarded the idea. She didn't care how famous he was, she did not know him well enough to invite him into her apartment.

"You can say whatever you came to say from where you are."

Her voice met empty static on the other end of the intercom.

A few moments later there was heavy knocking at her door. Paige covered her chest with her hand, her heart beating like a drum within her chest.

She cracked the door open, but left the chain on. He looked a thousand times better in person than he ever had on the cover of *Sports Illustrated*.

"How did you get up here?" she called.

"One of your neighbors let me in. She'll be back with her son's football card in a minute."

As if on cue, a woman she'd seen around the building approached. She gushed and fawned and pretty much made a fool of herself while Torrian signed a football card, a football, two magazine covers and a Sabers jersey.

When the woman finally left, he turned back to her door and leaned in close. "Can you please let me in before that happens again?" he asked.

"I'm not letting you into my apartment," she said.

"Why not?"

"Because I'm a single woman living in New York who understands the finer points of self-preservation," she returned.

"I'm not going to hurt you," he said in a voice that made her believe it. "I just want to talk. Our phone conversation didn't go so well, so I thought we could try a face-to-face." He held up his hands. "I promise I'm not here to do anything other than talk. I would never put my hands on a woman. Unless she asked," he added.

Paige studied him through the crack in the door. It *would* be pretty stupid of him to harm her, especially since thousands of people around the city had witnessed their heated debate on her blog.

"Fine," Paige relented. She closed the door and released the chain, opening it and stepping back to let him in.

Just as she'd been in Mancini's Grocery, she was momentarily awestruck by the sheer magnificence of the man standing before her. He towered at least a foot above her, and even though he was dressed in a pair of jeans and a pullover shirt, he exuded something that definitely made him different from the average man on the street.

"Thank you," he said as he stepped into her apartment, leaving a gentle wave of something subtle and spicy in his wake. She remembered it from their encounter in the produce section. The enticing aroma caused all manner of fluttery happenings within her stomach.

He walked over to her army green suede armchair and plopped down with an exhausted sigh.

"Make yourself at home," Paige snorted. She took a seat on the edge of her couch, crossed one leg over the other and rested her elbow on her knee.

"So?" she started.

Torrian dragged a hand down his face. His slightly almond-shaped hazel eyes held a hint of fatigue. He closed them, leaned his head on the back of her chair and expelled another sigh.

"Did you come here to take a nap?" Paige asked, intentionally heavy on the sarcasm.

He raised his head, cocked one eye open and had the nerve to grin. "I see the attitude extends beyond the blog."

Oh, good God, that grin was nice. He had a near-perfect face, with a mouth that eased into a decadent smile with zero effort. Paige had never realized the safety the TV screen provided until she was left without its protective barrier. Torrian Smallwood in the flesh was a very dangerous thing.

She had to clear her throat before speaking. "I know you didn't track me down to my home—which is the creepiest thing anyone has ever done, by the way—just to insult me yet again."

"If my saying you have attitude is an insult, you need to get some thicker skin, sweetheart."

Before she could call him on the *sweetheart* remark, he expelled another sigh and said, "This thing on your blog has gotten way out of hand."

"Only because you took it there," Paige responded. She reached over to her computer desk and caught the bowl of grapes with the tips of her fingers.

"I'm willing to own up to my part in this," Torrian said. He straightened in the chair and rested his elbows on his knees. "I shouldn't have responded, but I never intended for that first comment I posted to remain on the blog."

"Then why did you post it in the first place?" she asked. She held the bowl of grapes out for him. He picked off two and tossed them in his mouth.

Was she seriously sitting in her living room eating grapes with Torrian Smallwood? There was a sufficient amount of surrealism in the moment, but even more surreal was how comfortable it all felt. He was a superstar, but lounging in her favorite chair with fatigue in his eyes and contriteness in his voice, he could very well be any one of her friends. Or something more.

"Like I told you, it was a knee-jerk reaction. I know it was out of line and I apologized. You're the one who chose to ignore me and keep this thing public. Now we both look like fools."

"Only one of us looks like a fool, in my opinion. I've remained as professional as I possibly can."

He stared at her, his gaze assessing. "You're not as professional as you seem to think you are," he said.

Paige arched a brow. "Excuse me?"

"A true professional would have accepted my apology from the very beginning and erased my response last Sunday night. *You* decided to humiliate me on your blog instead."

"What apology?"

"Fine, maybe it wasn't an apology in the normal sense of the word."

"In *no* sense of the word," Paige returned.

"If you'd done what I'd asked in the first e-mail I sent Sunday night, there would be no reason for me to be in your apartment right now," Torrian said.

"You e-mailed me?"

"Several times," he nodded. "Starting with last Sunday. I explained that I was going to erase the comment I'd put on the blog but got distracted. I damn near begged you to go in and erase it, but you decided to ignore me."

He'd e-mailed her. Probably through her blog's e-mail, which she had not had a chance to check since Saturday night.

"I didn't see your e-mail," Paige admitted. She looked up at him, suffering the first twinge of regret she'd felt since this whole debacle first began. "I only check that e-mail account once a week."

His head fell back again as he let out a low groan. "You've gotta be kidding me. This could have all been prevented if you'd just read your e-mail."

"I'm not the one to blame here," Paige protested. "If you hadn't posted the response in the first place, this wouldn't be an issue."

He rested his elbows on his knees and clasped his hands between his spread legs. "You know what, none of it matters at this point. It's done. We need to figure out where to go from here."

"*We?* Exactly why do *we* need to figure out anything?" Paige asked.

"Because I don't want this thing to get any more out of hand than it already has," he said. He reached over and picked off another grape.

"I am not recanting my review," Paige declared.

He rolled his eyes heavenward. "Look, I get that you didn't like the book. You're entitled to your opinion. My main concern is that my fans will see me as someone who can't take a little criticism."

"Apparently, you *don't* take criticism well. This way your fans see the real you?"

"Paige." Her name came out of his mouth in a soft,

beseeching plea that caused a delicious ripple to cascade down Paige's spine. "That was not the real me," he said. "It's driving me crazy that people are getting this impression of me."

There was actual pain in his voice. Paige was puzzled by how seriously he was taking all of this. Sure, he'd look bad to a few fans, but he had millions of worshipers out there. Why should he care that a few thousand New Yorkers thought he was a jerk?

Paige settled back on the sofa and crossed her arms over her chest. "There is an easy way to fix this," she said.

His eyes flew to hers. "How?"

"You can write an apology on my blog," she stated.

"No way." Torrian shook his head. He shot up from the chair and walked over to the window that overlooked 3rd Avenue.

"Why not?" Paige asked, pushing up from the sofa so she could join him at the window.

Torrian turned to face her. He braced his legs apart and crossed his arms. "Because you would win," he answered, his voice cool, his eyes matching.

Paige's mouth gaped open. "You have *got* to be kidding me."

He took a step forward and settled a look on her that made the tiny hairs at the back of her neck stand on end. "I'm not going to roll over and play dead," he said. His eyes zeroed in. "I looked into you. You've built your career by cutting people down to size with your weekly column, and you're even worse on the blog. I'll be damned if I become one of your victims."

"Victim!" Paige laughed in his face. A bit of insanity seemed to accompany all that sexiness. "You've spent the past week attacking me on my own blog, but *you're* the victim?"

"I'm not apologizing," he stated.

"I'm not erasing anything from the Web site," she returned,

jutting her chin forward. He stood a hairbreadth away from her. The subtle heat radiating from his body caused a contradictory chill to skitter along Paige's skin. The man exuded sensuality by merely existing.

"I can go over your head," he said without a hint of smugness, just utter and complete certainty. "I'm sure I can convince the powers that be at *Big Apple Weekly* to listen to what I have to say."

Paige had no doubt Angie would back her up. The suits, however, were another story. The Pedlam brothers, Jory and Peter, who owned the paper, would probably side with Torrian for no reason other than he was a superstar they wanted to impress.

"Nearly two thousand people have already responded to the blog," Paige said. "Besides, I'm sure your response has been copied onto hundreds of other Web sites by now. Deleting it wouldn't make a bit of difference."

"You wouldn't have to delete anything," Torrian said.

Paige took a step back, needing distance between them as much as she needed her next breath. "What are you suggesting I do, if not delete everything?" she asked.

His shoulders had become rigid; the look in his eyes telling her that he'd been just as affected by their proximity. He broke eye contact, shaking his head and glancing out the window before turning back to her.

"I've been thinking about it since I called you," he started. "Instead of deleting any of our exchange, you can post another entry saying that we concocted this whole thing. Make it sound as if this was one big publicity stunt. The review, our arguing back and forth. All of it."

"My readers are much too smart to believe this entire thing has been a hoax," she explained.

"Maybe you give your readers more credit than they deserve."

"If you want to get on my good side, you'll cut back on the insults," Paige warned.

He groaned, ran a hand over his close-cut hair. "I'm not trying to insult you or your readers. I just think that if we really put our heads together, we can turn this whole thing around."

He reached out and grabbed her hand. Paige tried to jerk it away, but he held on tight. "You want an apology? Fine, I'm doing it right now. I'm sorry for ninety-nine percent of the stuff I said on your blog. I was pissed and I stepped over the line, but I *need* you to make this right, Paige."

The anguish in his plea caused the breath to catch in her throat. She looked up from where he grasped her hand, and was bowled over by the genuine distress in his hazel eyes.

"Please," he implored.

Shaking her head to spring herself from her dazed state, Paige managed to pull her hand from his.

"If—" She cleared her throat. "If I were to consider this, I still believe we'd have to come up with something more plausible than what you suggested."

He hunched his shoulders. "I'm all ears. What do you suggest?"

"I don't know," Paige admitted. "To be honest, I think this is all going to die in no time if we stop posting nasty responses to each other on the blog. I'm putting up my next review tomorrow. Once readers start discussing that one, yours will fade into the blackness."

He wasn't convinced. Paige could tell by the way he said, "How can you be so sure?"

She sent him a slight, wry grin. "Yours is not the first review to stir up a bit of controversy on my blog."

His cell phone rang. He took it from his pocket, glanced at the phone, then said, "Excuse me."

He turned away from her, back to the window. "What's up,

Dee?" A pause. "He didn't tell you where he was going?" she heard Torrian say in a troubled tone. It was a bit intrusive to stand here and listen, but she was in her own apartment. He'd brought his conversation here.

"I'll be there in a minute," he finished and ended the call.

He turned back to her, and Paige refused to look guilty for listening in. His furrowed brow and tightened lips compelled her to ask, "Is everything okay?"

"Can we finish this later, over dinner, maybe?" he asked as he started walking toward the door.

"I'm not going out with you," she said.

"Come on, Paige. I think we could do a better job of settling this if we did it over a nice meal."

"No," she returned. The intimacy such a setting would create started a mix of anxiety and anticipation churning in the pit of Paige's stomach. She *had* to keep things on a professional playing field where Torrian was concerned.

Still, Paige couldn't help but feel concern over the unease she sensed flowing over him. She followed him to the door. Without thinking, Paige grabbed his forearm, halting his retreat. "Is there anything I can do?"

He looked down at her hand clasping his arm, then back up at her. Something flashed in his eyes. It didn't take Paige but a second to recognize what it was. It was the same thing that was running through her own blood.

Hunger.

Instant, intense, burning hunger.

Electricity surged between them, holding her captive. The charged air made the skin on her arm pebble with goose bumps. She wanted to jerk her eyes away from his, but she couldn't. His molten gaze held her spellbound.

Finally Paige found the strength to release his arm. She took a step back, and they both swallowed long and deep.

"I...I'm sorry," she said, even though she didn't know what she was apologizing for. Who was at fault for the intense desire that had begun to thrum through the air the moment she touched him?

He took a step closer, and her breath seized in her throat. His cell phone rang again.

"Dammit," he whispered. His eyes bored into hers, filled with a heat so extreme it warmed her from the inside out. "I have to go," he said.

Without another word, he walked out of her apartment, closing the door behind him.

Chapter 7

Paige poured tea from the ornate teapot and sat it back onto the trivet in the center of the table. She was tired of drinking this darn tea. If Angela didn't get here in the next five minutes, she was going solo.

But not having the distraction of Angela and her fiancé to share in the dinner conversation left her mind open to explore other things. Like Torrian Smallwood's visit to her apartment. Having him there had been…well…nice. Too nice. So nice that it's all she had been able to think about.

His position as a wide receiver had lent to his perfect build. He had muscles for days, but they were lean, sinewy and just the right size. The power in his muscular legs had been displayed to perfection when he sat on her favorite green chair and the fabric of his expensive jeans had stretched taut over them. The man was a study in the perfect body.

She was safer having that perfect body on her television screen, not in the middle of her living room. He was just a bit too tempting, and a stark reminder of a basic missing element in her life.

It had been over two years since she'd had what could be even remotely called a serious boyfriend, and to be honest, there was nothing serious about her relationship with Michael Weston. He'd started out as a coworker at her first job with a small paper in New York, and they had soon become friends. A few months later it had turned into something more, but neither of them had any illusions that what they shared would lead to something permanent. Michael had told her in his last e-mail that he had just proposed to his old girlfriend. Paige was happy for him.

Her cell phone chimed the tune she had designated for Angela.

"You'd better have a good excuse for being so late," Paige barked into the phone.

"I'm in the hospital," Angela answered.

"What?" Paige shrieked, causing more than a few heads to turn. "Are you okay?"

"I'm fine. It's Bryce. He was trying to trim roses he bought to surprise me. I'm really sorry, Paige. I know this is the second time I've stood you up."

"Well, it couldn't really be helped this time," she answered. "Tell Bryce I hope he feels better."

"Thanks, Paige. If the food is any good, maybe we can go again next week. My treat."

"I'm not holding my breath," Paige laughed.

"I totally deserve that," Angela chuckled. "I'll talk to you tomorrow."

Paige disconnected and sighed. She was used to eating alone; she didn't know why the prospect seemed so bleak now. She motioned for the table attendant. She didn't need to occupy such a large table now.

"May I help you, ma'am?" the attendant asked.

"The rest of my party couldn't make it," Paige said. "Can I move to one of the smaller tables in the corner?"

"Of course," the girl answered. She gathered the teapot and trivet from the table. "I will bring you more tea."

"No, no more tea," Paige answered. "Actually, you can bring me a drink menu once I'm seated."

"Of course. Right this way, ma'am."

Paige rose from the table of four and followed the table attendant. Her step stuttered as she spotted Torrian heading straight toward her.

"Oh, God," she muttered. *Of all the sushi restaurants in New York...*

And, of course, the table attendant was guiding her directly in his path. There would be no escaping him. She could only hope he would ignore her as he made his way to his table.

She should have known better.

He stopped yards away and waited for her. "Good evening," he greeted as Paige approached.

"Hello, Mr. Smallwood," Paige said, her voice as unaffected as she could possibly expect it to be considering the situation.

"C'mon, Paige. I think there's enough history between us to be on a first-name basis by now," he said with that smile that made her stomach tremble and skin get all tingly.

"I don't know. I kind of like some of the other names I've been calling you," Paige said.

He barked a laugh. "I definitely don't want to hear any of those." He leaned in and said with a stage whisper, "Unless they're really dirty."

She shouldn't engage in this back-and-forth with him, but she found it hard not to fall into the playful tit for tat. "Oh, they are pretty dirty," Paige said. "Not the way you think, though."

His smile widened, and there was a definite weakening of her knees.

"If you don't mind, I was just about to have dinner," Paige said.

He looked to the table attendant, who'd been standing there watching their exchange with interest. Paige considered deducting a few points from her review of the restaurant for having a nosy waitstaff.

"Are you dining alone?" Torrian asked.

"I am now," she answered honestly.

"Would you mind some company?" he asked.

"*You're* alone?" The question escaped her mouth before she could temper her surprised tone.

"The last time I took my sister and nephew out for sushi, it didn't go over too well," he answered, and with a shrug continued, "I've been eyeing this place for a while and decided to finally give it a try. After turning down all my invitations to dinner, I can only assume this is fate stepping in."

In her book, what he was doing qualified as flirting, but Paige wasn't sure the same rules applied to charmers with the professional expertise Torrian possessed. She'd seen him unleash that smile on enough fans and reporters to know that reading anything more into it would be a faux pas on her part.

But what about that…*something* that had passed between them before he left her apartment? Tremors of excitement rippled along her skin whenever she thought about his heated gaze. It made her wonder what would have happened if his cell phone had not interrupted them. Would he have left her apartment? Would she have let him?

"So, Paige, can I join you for dinner?" He leaned just a bit more toward her, and lowered his voice. "Maybe we can finish what we were discussing yesterday."

Which part? she wanted to ask.

Over the course of the half hour he'd been at her apartment, the air surrounding their discussion had traveled along a spectrum of intimacy that still caused Paige's breath to hitch. She went from not wanting to invite him into her home, to suffering a moment of sadness when he'd had to leave. How was that even possible?

"For two?" the table attendant asked, an expectant, excited look on her face.

"For two," Torrian said, and Paige didn't refute him.

They were guided to a table in a corner, which is what she'd asked for, Paige remembered. It certainly had a different connotation to it now. The attendant waited until they were seated, then presented them with menus. "I will get the drink menu you requested," she said before leaving.

Paige nodded her thanks, then turned her attention to her new dinner guest. "Did everything turn out okay?" she asked. "You left in a hurry last night."

He waved away her concern. "My nephew is going through a knucklehead phase. Skipping class, missing curfew, driving his mom crazy. She's convinced it's something more than typical teenage stuff, so I had a little heart-to-heart with Dante last night. It's all good." Torrian opened his menu. "I've heard some good things about this place. The shrimp tempura is supposed to be excellent."

"I hope so," Paige said. "I've been impressed with the atmosphere so far. If the food lives up to the hype, it'll make things a lot easier." At his confused looked, Paige clarified, "I'm reviewing the restaurant for my next column."

"Ah," Torrian sat back. "I hope they know not to get on your bad side." His grin was rueful, but Paige thought she caught a bit of self-deprecation. "I'm sorry," he said, "I couldn't help it."

She felt the need to defend herself. "Negative reviews are not my default."

"I shouldn't have said any—"

"People seem to think—"

The attendant returned with the drink menu, interrupting Paige's rebuttal. They ordered sake for two and two bottles of mineral water.

When the attendant left, Paige continued, determined to make her point. "I don't go into a review hoping to find things to complain about," she said.

"I know that," Torrian said.

"It feels as if I'm getting a reputation for being this ball-busting—"

"Please," he stopped her, reaching over the small round table and covering her hand with his. "What I said was uncalled for. I can't seem but to stick my foot in my mouth when I'm around you," he said. "I'm sorry."

Her skin burned where he touched it. Her entire body warmed with him so close. "We have gotten off to a rocky start," Paige agreed, pulling her hand away in an effort to preserve her sanity.

"I'm not the jerk I appear to be."

"Don't worry," Paige laughed. "You're not the first person to accuse me of bringing out the worse in them."

"It's not you, it's this entire situation. Any confrontation I experience usually remains on the football field. I'm not good at handling it off the field. I guess I need to practice my diplomacy skills."

He smiled, and her stomach tightened. She'd seen him enough times on television and magazines to understand that there was something about Torrian Smallwood that went beyond what other men possessed, but to be inundated with that raw, in-your-face sexual magnetism was overwhelming.

"You should have more practice at this diplomacy thing than I do. You said yourself that I'm not the first person who's caused some strife on your blog."

"No, you're not," she answered. The people at Goldstein Publishing were probably ready to put a hit out on her.

"So, what's the deal?" He leaned forward and settled his elbows on the table. "Why did you chew me out on your blog? What do you have against me, Paige?"

"I don't have anything against you," Paige insisted. "My review was not personal. When I read a book, or see a show, or eat at a restaurant, I have a certain set of criteria in mind, and your book did not live up to those criteria. It's as simple as that."

"So are you saying none of that stuff you posted on your blog was personal?" Torrian asked.

"It wasn't supposed to be," she said. "I did take a couple of cheap shots, though. I apologize for that. But you did the same," she pointed out to make herself feel better.

"I know." He shook his head, staring at a spot on the table. When he looked up at her, genuine remorse shone in his honey-colored eyes. "I really am sorry for some of the things I said." A rueful smile edged up the corner of his mouth as he toyed with the packets of artificial sweeteners on the table. "I pride myself on setting a good example for my nephew of how to be respectful of women, and here I am, doing the complete opposite."

Paige leaned over and caught his hand. "Stop beating yourself up. I accept your apology."

As soon as she touched him, something changed. His eyes slowly traveled from where their hands touched up to her eyes. His thumb caressed the underside of her wrist, moving back and forth across the sensitive spot.

The table attendant returned with their drinks, and Paige pulled her hand away. What was it that passed between them every time they touched? The mystifying current of electricity had continued to thrum through her body long after he'd left her apartment, and the same was happening again. Her wrist tingled where he'd touched it.

"Have you decided on what you would like for dinner?" the waitress asked.

Paige asked Torrian about his preferences, but he conceded the ordering to her. She ordered shrimp tempura, a platter of assorted sashimi and a spicy yellowtail roll.

"So," Torrian asked. "What are we going to do about the blog?"

"I've been considering your proposition from the other day."

"You agree that we should just say this was one big publicity stunt?"

"Yes…and no," she said. She stopped him before he could say anything. "Pulling this 'publicity stunt' may be acceptable in your line of work, but not for me. I would lose credibility with my readers if they thought my review was part of some big hoax to drum up attention for your book. I can't allow that to happen."

"So what do you suggest?" he asked. Their food arrived in record time, and Torrian dived in, using his chopsticks to expertly lift a sliver of raw tuna from the rectangular dish.

"I'm not completely sure yet," Paige answered honestly. She dipped the tempura in soy sauce. "I still believe this will die down soon. Now that we're no longer fueling the flames with our remarks, interests will wane."

"Don't you think I'll still need to do some damage control?" Torrian asked.

"How much of a hit do you think your reputation has taken because of this?" she asked. Although it shouldn't matter to her in the least, Paige didn't like the thought of people not liking him because of what had transpired on her blog over the past few days.

He shrugged. "I'm not sure." He placed the chopsticks on

his plate and wiped his mouth with a napkin. He had a set of the most decadent lips imaginable. Same went for his eyes. "There have been a lot of comments on your blog," he said.

"Yeah, but not all of them have been bad. Your die-hard fans have stood up for you. And when you think about the number of fans you have around this city, those comments on my blog are only a drop in the bucket."

"The thought of even one fan being disappointed in the way I behaved on your blog is too many for me," he said.

"I'm impressed that you care so much," she admitted. "At first, I thought it was all about your book and restaurant; that you didn't want fans to think negatively of you because it would affect your sales."

His eyes softened. "At the risk of losing the drop of respect I seem to have earned from you, I'll admit that the book and restaurant factor into it."

His honesty had the opposite effect. Between his visit to her apartment and their conversation here, her opinion of him had changed dramatically.

"Can I ask you something?" Paige asked, using one chopstick to stir up the bowl of sashimi dipping sauce. "You have a successful football career. Why is the success of this book so important to you?"

"It's not so much the book; it's the restaurant. It is my sister's dream."

"The sister you mention in the book? The one who raised you?"

He nodded. "I owe Deirdre everything. She sacrificed her future to make a better one for me. This restaurant is the one thing she's always wanted. It scares the hell out of me to think that her dream could be crushed because of all of this."

His concern wasn't for himself, but for his sister. Paige's heart melted then and there.

"And here I thought you were a jerk," she said, allowing her own grin to travel along her lips.

"I don't like the thought of you thinking I'm a jerk. If you give me a chance, I'd like to prove to you that I'm not."

Paige's breath caught somewhere in her throat. The zing that had only occurred when they touched hit her again, and this time it spread all over her body.

His voice, when he spoke, was low. Seductive. "Will you let me prove that to you, Paige?"

She tried to speak, but the words would not surface.

"Excuse me, Mr. Smallwood?"

At the interruption, they both snapped to attention. Paige wasn't sure if she should be disappointed or relieved.

Two girls, who couldn't be more than sixteen years old, held out napkins. "Can we please have your autograph?" they asked in unison.

Torrian turned his attention to his fans, smiling up at them both. For the first time, Paige noticed a difference. The smile on his face now was indulgent; it didn't encompass his whole face the way it had when he'd smile at her. This was his game face. He'd given her the real thing.

When he'd signed the napkins and taken pictures with both girls on their camera phones, he turned back to her. "Sorry about that."

Paige waved off his concern with a flick of her chopsticks, deciding it was for the best that they had been interrupted. "It's to be expected. I'm not sure how much I'd want your life," Paige said. "I like my privacy."

"You have a fair amount of fame yourself."

"Not really, you hadn't heard of me before this all happened." She grinned.

"No, I hadn't," he said, "But apparently I'm the exception, if the number of people who read your blog is any indication."

Paige shrugged. "There's a measure of anonymity in

writing for the paper. I like that I can let my voice be heard but maintain a low profile. This situation with you has given me a bit more attention than I'm used to." She felt the smile tipping up the corner of her mouth. "I have to admit to enjoying it just a little."

"Happy I could help with that," he said, his voice a mixture of amusement and heat.

"Um, Torrian? What's happening here?" Paige asked as nonchalantly as she could. Her heart rate had been on continual escalation mode since the moment he'd reached over and traced his fingers along hers.

"We're having dinner," he answered, that smile still on his face, his voice still as seductive as a candlelit dinner with champagne and strawberries.

"You know what I mean," she said. "Just a day ago we were mortal enemies."

He stared at her, the look in his eyes intensifying. "Of all the things I'd like to be to you, your enemy is dead last on the list." The lone candle flickering from the small blue bowl in the center of the table cast a shadow across his strong, smooth jaw. "You feel this," he said, the words low, seductive, intense. "I feel you shiver every time I touch you."

Paige tried to speak but couldn't. She wanted to deny his words, but how could she when they washed over her with such delicious warmth? She *did* feel it. This buzz of sexuality pulling between them, as if they were two magnets trying desperately to meet, but being pushed apart by the discord between them.

"We shouldn't feel this," Paige said. "We… This isn't right."

Torrian captured her hand. "What's not right about it?"

Paige jerked her hand away, but her eyes were still imprisoned by his deep, dark gaze. "What about everything that's been said?" she reasoned. "I can't go from despising you one minute to…to not despising you the next."

"You already have," he said. "Can't we just agree that we jumped to the wrong conclusions about each other before really getting to know one another?"

"We don't know each other now."

"I want to change that."

"Why?" she asked, hating the pleading in her voice.

"Because I want to know you, Paige. I'm attracted to you." He pushed the platter of sashimi to the side and caught her other hand. "We're attracted to each other," he amended. "Whether it's just physical, I'm not sure, but don't you think we owe it to ourselves to figure that out?"

Paige's first instinct was to deny that what she felt for him was attraction, but how could she when her skin still tingled where he'd held her hand?

"How would it look if after spending the past week and a half engaged in verbal swordplay with you on my blog, we all of a sudden ended up being seen together?"

"No one has to know." His intense stare stole her breath away. "Come on, Paige," Torrian continued. "Tell me you don't feel this."

She couldn't. As much as she wanted to deny it, her conscience would not allow her to voice such a lie.

But just because she felt this attraction, it didn't mean she was willing to explore it. Her professional reputation was at stake. She'd busted her butt to make a name for herself on her own merit. She would not be accused of riding the coattails of a celebrity.

"I can't do this," she said. She pulled her hand from his and pushed away from the table. "Don't worry about dinner. The restaurant is picking up the tab."

"Paige, wait," Torrian said. He stood up, grabbing her arm.

They stood so close their bodies touched. The heat radiating off him was as hot as molten lava.

"No one has to know," he repeated.

Paige closed her eyes. Every cell in her body screamed for her to say yes. He was the object of millions of fantasies, and he was interested in *her*. She would be a fool to turn down his invitation to see where this fire-hot attraction could take them.

But she had to.

She shook her head. "I'm sorry," was all she could manage before pulling away and escaping the restaurant.

Chapter 8

Paige's fingers flew across the keyboard as she put the finishing touches on this week's column. The sushi restaurant had been a hit, despite her cowardly escape from Torrian. Unfortunately, the off-Broadway show she'd attended last night needed to scoot a little further off Broadway. The playwright was not ready for the big time.

Paige clicked into her e-mail again. "Come on, Angela," she said. She'd been waiting to get the okay from Angela to post her next review, but couldn't wait any longer. Seconds after she hit the button to post the review, she got the approval.

"A bit late," Paige murmured. She hoped the review would help curb her readers' obsession with this Torrian Smallwood thing. Their online sparring match had been a nice boost to her readership, but it was time for it to end. The disquiet she'd sensed in Torrian had been real. He was genuinely concerned about what this was doing to his reputation, and the impact it could have on the restaurant he was so generously opening so his sister could live out her dream.

It was hard to ignore the tug on her heart every time she recalled the sincerity she'd witnessed in his eyes.

She went into the kitchen to make tea. As she reached for the honey, Paige noticed something familiar in the corner of her eye. She turned to the television. Her picture from the blog shared a split screen with a picture of Torrian in a Sabers uniform. Paige dived for the remote and raised the volume.

"...the most heated exchange the Fire Starter has ever had. Local entertainment columnist Paige Turner shows she isn't star-struck by the Sabers star player. When it comes to her book reviews, Ms. Turner is an equal opportunity attacker."

"You have got to be kidding me," Paige groaned. She folded her arms on the bar and dropped her head on them. Making the evening news was *not* going to help in burying Torrian's review.

She was itching to check the site statistics on her blog, but she had to get ready for the weekly staff meeting at *Big Apple Weekly.* Paige turned off the fire under the tea kettle and left her teacup sitting on the counter untouched. She quickly dressed and twenty minutes later, walked into the offices at *Big Apple Weekly.*

"They're meeting in the smaller conference room," Veronica, the receptionist, informed her.

As she walked down the hallway, Paige noticed the larger conference room was stacked with boxes. Kaydie, the intern, and Mitchell, the lead Web designer, were sitting at the table in the smaller conference room when Paige entered.

"What's going on?" She pointed toward the other conference room.

"Peter's wife threw him out again," Mitchell answered, his

eyes never leaving the screen of his laptop. Peter Pedlam's wife threw him out of the house at least twice a year.

"Your blog has been getting major traffic," Kaydie said to Paige.

"Yes, I know," Paige answered. "Although I'm not sure how good all this attention is."

"Any attention is good attention."

Angela entered the room, quickly followed by the other half of the Pedlam brothers, Jory, who, by all accounts, had a fairly stable relationship with his wife.

"Peter won't be joining us," Jory said by way of greeting.

"We figured," Mitchell said, still staring at the computer.

It took less than twenty minutes to go through the weekly staff meeting's normal agenda.

Jory turned his attention to Paige. "Lastly, I received a call from KWEZ, Channel 10. They have a proposal for a news segment featuring Paige."

Paige sat up straight. "What kind of proposal?"

"They want to bring you and Torrian together on their show. They'd like to meet with us tomorrow."

Paige shook her head. "I don't know about that, Jory." How was she supposed to bury this thing with Torrian if people kept bringing it up?

"Don't be so quick to say no. I think it's in the best interest of both you and *Big Apple Weekly* to at least listen to what they propose."

Anytime Jory used the in-the-best-interest line, Paige knew he'd pretty much made up his mind on the subject. She needed to convince him otherwise.

"Jory, this thing with the Smallwood book has gotten way out of hand. I'd rather it die a natural death than to continue fueling the fire by appearing on the news."

Jory gave her a peculiar look. "I'm not saying you have to do it, but you should listen to what they have to say." He addressed the rest of the room's occupants. "That's all for now."

"Jory, can I speak with you?" Paige called before he could follow the others.

Her boss turned with his hands up. "This can be a good thing, Paige. Just trust me," he said.

"Are you kidding me? Have you even read the back-and-forth between us on the blog?"

"Yes, I have."

"And yet you can say this could be a good thing with a straight face? Impressive, Jory."

"Paige, just…" Jory's jaw twitched. "Look, you are at a pivotal point in your career. Trust me when I say you *want* to see this through."

There was something in his voice that caught Paige's attention. "What's going on?"

His eyes widened in feigned surprised, but he didn't do the innocent act well.

"Fess up," Paige said.

"Fine, but if this falls through, you only have yourself to blame for being disappointed. There's talk of syndication," Jory continued. He put his hands up, staving off her inquiry. "I don't have specifics yet, so don't even ask. But yes, there has been talk."

The air in the room seemed to dry up instantaneously. Paige was so shocked she could hardly breathe.

She'd been happy writing for *Big Apple Weekly* these past few years, but her goal—as with any journalist—had always been to see her name in print in a major paper. Paige knew syndication of her entertainment column was a huge jump in the direction of a columnist position with one of the bigger papers. Her blood began to pump faster just at the thought.

"That's why I want you to meet with KWEZ tomorrow,"

Jory continued. "This can be a huge move for you, career-wise."

"Whatever *this* is," Paige said. "What if whatever the station suggests makes me look like a fool?"

"Any buzz you can generate would be a mark in the plus column."

Jory was right. It was all about exposure. That was the whole point of being syndicated, to expose as many readers to her writing as she could.

Good God. *Syndication*. Paige could hardly wrap her brain around it.

"What time is tomorrow's meeting?" she asked Jory.

Her boss smiled. "Eleven a.m. I'll see you there."

Torrian entered through the revolving glass door of the building on West 57th. KWEZ Channel 10 was on the twenty-eighth floor. It took him and his agent, David Sage, a full ten minutes to make it across the atrium to the bank of elevators. Even businessmen had kids who wanted autographs.

"You ever get tired of that?" David asked with a sly grin as he held open the door to a surprisingly empty elevator car.

Torrian shrugged. "Comes with the territory."

"Hold the elevator, please," came a voice he'd been hearing in his dreams.

Paige Turner, flanked on either side by men in business suits, appeared in the open elevator door. Torrian experienced the same jolt of sensation that shocked his system whenever he occupied the same space with her. What was it about this woman that caused his heart rate to go from zero to sixty in less than a second?

He moved to the side and gave her a gentlemanly nod. "Good morning, Ms. Turner."

She walked into the elevator. "Good morning to you, Mr. Smallwood."

Damn, her voice was sexy, and she smelled like lemon and some type of flower. He didn't know which one, but it was soft and sweet and perfect for her.

One of her flankers jutted his hand out. "Torrian, how are you doing? Jory Pedlam." He gestured to the second guy. "This is my brother Peter. We're co-owners of *Big Apple Weekly*."

"Nice to meet you both," Torrian answered. He turned so he could bring Paige into his line of vision. He wanted to *see* her. "I've learned a lot about your magazine over the past couple of weeks." He gestured toward David. "This is my agent, David Sage."

"Ah, yes," Peter Pedlam said. "You've scored some major clients in the past couple of years."

"None as big as number eighty-eight here," Jory put in.

Torrian noticed Paige's eye roll. Obviously, she wasn't as impressed by David's client list as her bosses.

He leaned closer and said in a low voice, "How are you doing this morning?"

"Just fine," she answered. "Curious as to what this is all about."

"So am I," he agreed. In fact, Torrian had debated whether he should even be here. The media, for the most part, had been kind to him. But they could turn on you in an instant. David had badgered the producer who'd called to set up this meeting, but all he could pry out of her was that they wanted to discuss a charity fundraiser revolving around Paige and Torrian's blog war.

On the twenty-eighth floor they were immediately greeted by a guy in khakis and a polo-style shirt with the KWEZ logo on the breast pocket. He led them into a conference room. In one corner was a bar with two coffee carafes, pitchers of both orange juice and iced water, and a basket of pastries.

The men waited for Paige to take her seat. Her eyes roamed

around the table. "Oh, please. Just sit down," she said. She leveled Peter and Jory with a glare. "I've told you both before that all this chivalrous stuff freaks me out. I'm used to two brothers who both would pull my hair and slip frogs under my bed sheets."

"So, that's where you learned to hold your own when you're up against the big boys?" Jory laughed.

"Yes, it is," Paige answered. "I had more practice than I should have."

A brunette outfitted in a blazer with the same KWEZ logo and a pair of jeans entered the room. "Good morning," she said. "I'm Chelsea Robert, the station manager here at KWEZ. Before we get started, can John get you anything to eat or drink?"

The Pedlam brothers both requested black decaf and donuts. David asked for juice. Torrian accepted a glass of water. Paige declined any food or drink.

He was having a hard time reading her mood. Over the course of their meal, Torrian had been sure he had been making progress, but her abrupt departure had been a serious blow to his confidence. He couldn't be sure of anything where Paige was concerned. Maybe he'd moved too fast. As she'd pointed out at dinner, they had been mortal enemies just a few days ago.

Torrian had never considered her his enemy. He wasn't sure where she stood, but he knew where he wanted to be. Anywhere. With her. Spending time getting to know her.

As the refreshments were passed around the table, Chelsea Robert started, "Well, you two have made quite the entertaining pair on your blog. It would make for fascinating television."

"Which, I assume, is why we're here," Torrian interjected. He glanced over at Paige. Her eyes were focused on the station manager.

That soft skin of hers looked even softer this morning. His hand tingled in delicious remembrance of the way her skin had felt.

"We would like to bring your blog battle onto our set in the form of a cook-off." Chelsea Robert motioned to him. "In your post-game interview after the Tampa Bay game, you issued a challenge to Paige. You said if she had any questions regarding your cooking ability, you would meet her in the kitchen to see who the better cook was. Well, we want to provide the kitchen."

"You want us to cook together on live TV?" Paige asked, a bubble of disbelief in her voice.

"Against each other." Excitement danced in Chelsea's eyes. "Five courses over the next five weeks. The best part is that the people at Meyer cookware have agreed to sponsor the cook-off. The winner of each round gets a $20,000 prize to award to the charity of their choice."

"And all we have to do is cook?" Paige asked, the same skepticism in her eyes coming through her voice.

"Cook, and keep up the little sparring match the two of you have been engaged in on your blog."

"It would have to take place before my restaurant opens," Torrian said.

"Actually, it would have to take place *after* I agree to it," Paige corrected him.

So they were back to this.

Torrian could only shake his head as he looked over at her. The woman fed off being difficult the way a vampire fed off blood. She just looked much better doing it.

He drilled her with his stare, *So this is how we're going to play this?*

Her answering gaze gave a resounding *Yes.*

"What could be your objection to winning a portion of a hundred thousand dollars for your favorite charity?" Torrian asked. "Unless you doubt your ability to win even one round," he tacked on with a grin.

"Don't even go there," Paige answered. "We all know you didn't come up with a single one of those recipes. Tell me, Torrian, do you even know how to turn on a stove?"

God, she was sexy when she was being difficult. "Don't fool yourself, Ms. Turner. I know my way around the kitchen."

"Just enough to set it on fire," Paige returned. "That hilarious little story was about the only entertaining part of your book."

Torrian covered his chest with his hand. "Score one for you."

"Thank you." Paige inclined her head.

Torrian remembered the room's other occupants. Everyone else at the table had become completely silent.

"Please continue," the station manager begged.

"No need," Torrian said. "I'm in." He sat back in his chair and pressed his lips against his steepled fingers, waiting for Paige to make the next move.

She settled back in her chair. Her short hairstyle framed her delicate ears, and those high, regal cheekbones made her seem as if she were a descendant of African royalty. All eyes were on her, but she handled the pressure with aplomb. A slight smile tipped up her delicately shaped lips.

"I've never been one to back down from a challenge," she said.

Chelsea Robert's eyes beamed brighter than the lights above Sabers Stadium. "This is going to be television gold," she smiled. She pressed a few buttons on a remote control and a screen on the wall and camera above head lowered simultaneously. She pressed a few more buttons and a calendar littered with colorful blocks illuminated the screen.

"We would like the segments to run as one of our Friday features. With you now being on injured reserve, we don't have to worry about the games interfering, right?" She directed her question to Torrian.

He nodded.

"Excellent. We cleared the seven forty-two spot. The first segment will run this coming Friday. Is that okay with you, Paige?"

Paige shrugged a shoulder. "My schedule is a lot more flexible than Mr. Smallwood's. Feel free to plan everything around his."

"Now that I'm out for the next five weeks, I'm just as flexible as you are. As long as I'm available for the Tuesday afternoon team meetings, it's all good," he said.

"Perfect," Chelsea proclaimed. "We just did a major remodel of our kitchen here in the studio, so this is a great way to debut our new look. We'd like to bring you two in tomorrow to shoot a couple of promo spots, if that's okay."

"Is there any way to do them today?" Torrian asked. He had an ophthalmologist appointment tomorrow, and God only knew what shape his eyes would be in after Latoya filled them with her array of drops.

"We could," Chelsea said. "The sooner the better. I would start the promos during prime-time tonight. Of course, if that's okay with you, Paige." They all looked over at her.

"I'm not really ready to go in front of a camera," Paige said, smoothing her hand over her perfectly styled hair.

This was just for show, Torrian decided. The woman had to know she looked amazing.

"We have a full hair and makeup staff," Chelsea said. "The spots really won't take all that long to shoot. We'll outfit you both in aprons, throw a few pots on the stove, and shoot only one or two close-ups. We'll be done in an hour tops."

"Today would be my only day," Torrian said. "I'm booked up for the rest of the week."

Paige shot him an indulgent smile. She was up one round

in their little game, and Torrian knew she wasn't about to lose her advantage.

"Fine," she said. She unclasped her hands and pushed away from the table. "Show me to hair and makeup."

Chapter 9

Paige tried to stop her heart's chaotic beating, but she couldn't expect to actually be calm at a time like this. She absolutely despised being in front of the camera. That's one of the reasons she chose to be a writer. Writers were heard, not seen.

Think about syndication, Paige reminded herself.

She chanted the phrase over and over again as she followed the station manager.

"Hair and makeup will meet you in here in just a few minutes," Chelsea said. "When you're done in makeup, John will bring you to the kitchen set."

As Chelsea left the room, Torrian swiveled the chair he'd sat in and asked, "So, are we back to being mortal enemies?"

His words from dinner had played over and over again in her mind. He'd admitted to being attracted to her, and she was certainly attracted to him. The thought of pursuing anything, even a let's-just-get-to-know-each-other-better thing with him was more than a little tempting.

But the price was too high.

To be seen on Torrian's arm just when she was about to be syndicated would cast doubt on everything she'd worked so hard to attain.

"I've given some thought to what you suggested over dinner," Paige started.

"Which suggestion?" he asked, his grin nearly impossible to resist.

"That we…um, acknowledge this," she waved a hand between them, "this thing that seems to be humming between us."

"C'mon, Paige, you have to admit it's more than just a hum. We've got a full-blown choir singing around us."

"Fine." Paige held her hands up. "Still, I think things should remain professionally courteous between us and nothing more."

His brow dipped into deep vee. "Why?" he asked, the one word soaked in disappointment.

"For several reasons," she said, "Most important being that you're too high profile for my taste. The extra traffic to my blog has been nice, but I'm not looking to become a permanent fixture on *Entertainment Tonight*."

"So why did you agree to do this?" He motioned around the makeup room.

Paige wasn't about to tell him about the potential syndication deal, which was definitely her catalyst for agreeing to stand before a camera when there was absolutely nothing she'd least rather do. She decided to tell him a partial truth.

"It was the money for charity that cinched the deal," she said.

"You've already picked a charity?"

She nodded. "The Artist Medical Fund. It's an organization that provides low-cost medical insurance to artists, musicians and writers, among others in the liberal arts who are self-employed and can't afford private insurance."

He nodded his head. "A worthy cause," he said. "I may have to throw one of the competitions on purpose."

Paige barked a laugh.

"You really think you can win this competition?" Torrian asked.

"Absolutely," Paige stated with a confidence she didn't feel.

"Don't let this NFL player persona fool you." He grinned. "I grew up in the South, sugar. Cooking is in my blood. The food you all cook up here in New York is good and all, but it can't touch the old-fashioned soul food I grew up eating in South Carolina."

Paige leaned back in her chair and crossed her arms over her chest. Thinking about her family back in New Orleans, which was way farther south and much better known for its cooking than South Carolina, Paige said, "I guess I should be scared then, huh?"

"I think so," he said. He leaned forward in the chair, and in a hushed voice, said, "Not to give away all of my secrets, but I've got a slight advantage here."

"Oh, really? And what is that?"

"My sister, Deirdre."

"I'll take that into consideration, but since you're the one who has to do the actual cooking, I'm not too worried."

"You've been warned." His grin was sexy and infuriating at the same time, but Paige had to admit to enjoying the banter. "So, tell me how you really feel about this competition?" he asked.

"Other than being more than confident that I'm going to win?" Paige asked with a sweet smile.

Just as he was about to reply, the double doors opened and two young women came through. Of course, they both fawned over Torrian. Paige was surprised they didn't flip a coin to see who would win the honor of doing his makeup.

John, the guy who'd first greeted them when they came to the station, appeared just as the makeup artists were completing their task. Paige's face felt stiff as a board. The most makeup she wore was a swipe of lip gloss and some eyeliner. It was another perk of being the unseen face of her column.

The stylist did a few last-minute curls with the curling iron, and squeezed her shoulders. "Okay, you're done," she said.

"We're all set?" John asked.

"I am." Paige turned to find Torrian staring. His eyes traveled from the top of her head to the tips of her toes in a blatantly interested perusal. He remained quiet, but that look had said enough. He was not giving up this quest to "get to know her better." Paige swallowed deep while her blood pressure spiked.

He gestured to the open door. "You first," he said, his soft voice the equivalent of brushed velvet rubbing along her skin.

They followed John down yet another hallway and onto a darkened set. He switched on a light. Several spotlights shone down on a kitchen set outfitted with stainless steel appliances and contemporary colors.

Clipboard still in hand, John held a finger to his lips. He pointed to a blue partition. "The noon newscast is just next door," he whispered. "They should be done in a second." Moments later, upbeat, instrumental music came through the partition.

"Great, they're done." John moved to the area between the two kitchen islands, both with stovetops and a single sink. "Paige, you'll have the one on the right."

Paige moved around to the other side of the island and trailed her fingers along the range top, feeling like a perpetrator. She grew up in a family full of cooks—her grandparents had owned a Creole restaurant and her mother and aunts all grew up cooking their parents' recipes. With all those cooks in the kitchen, she had never felt the pressure to join them. Sure, she could throw together a meal when she had to, but a gourmet chef she was not.

"You look as if you're already thinking of ways to take me down."

"You're not the only one who knows something about game plans," Paige answered.

"Maybe I underestimated you." He laughed.

He had such a beautiful laugh. It was natural, not the fake chuckle she equated with most celebrity types.

The partition separating the kitchen from the news desk was moved back a few feet.

"Are we ready in here?" A guy wearing a headset came in, followed by two others. They pulled out the large cameras that were tucked away in a corner and placed them about a dozen feet in front of the two cooking stations.

"Your lines will be on the teleprompter," Headset guy said.

"Lines?" Paige groaned. Wasn't it enough that she had to be in front of the camera? They expected her to speak as well?

"Only a few," the director said.

Torrian leaned over, his mouth tipped up in a grin that was too sexy for words. "Don't tell me you're camera shy?"

Paige sighed. It's not as if she could ever hide her stage fright. She still had nightmares over that fourth-grade Christmas play. When you had a hard time reading the script, it only made reciting it that much more difficult. "Public speaking is not my forte," she admitted.

"The trick is to imagine there's just one person out there who's going to see it. I always pretend I'm speaking to my sister when I'm talking about something light and fun, and my old guidance counselor when I need to be serious. Mrs. Green had this personal vendetta against people who smiled."

"Are we ready?" Headset Guy asked.

They both got into position. The lights along the room's perimeter were shut off, and at least five additional spotlights shone down on them. The heat was instantaneous.

"You'll get used to the temperature," the director called, as if he'd read Paige's mind. Paige wasn't sure what caused the sweat: the glaring spotlights, the thought of speaking in front of a camera or the sexy football player standing less than eight feet away.

That he was gorgeous was a given. Torrian Smallwood was one of those sex symbols who'd transcended the football field and had infiltrated other areas of entertainment.

And if it turned out he *did* know his way around the kitchen? Good Lord, some things were just too hard to resist.

"And we're rolling," the director said.

"What? Huh?" Paige looked up at the camera.

"Cut," the director said.

Oh, great. Not the best start to her big television debut.

"You know what?" the director said, "I think it would work better if Torrian started out first. Give me a minute." He went to a computer set up just to the right of the camera that wasn't in use and began typing.

"Remember what I told you?" Paige jumped back in surprise at Torrian's voice right over her shoulder. She hadn't even heard him move away from his station.

"Who are you most comfortable talking to?" he asked.

"Ah…my coworker, Angela."

"Okay, pretend it's just Angela out there. You're speaking only to her."

"I know. I'm sorry," she said. "I wasn't ready." Because she'd been thinking about him.

"Torrian, we'll start with you," the director said. "Let's see how this first run goes, and if you two need to take a break to learn the lines, we can take ten minutes."

"We've got this. Right?" He looked over at her. His voice had softened and his eyes were filled with a concern that was as sweet as it was unnerving. Why couldn't he go back to being the hostile guy who'd attacked her on her blog? She was prepared to deal with that guy. What Paige wasn't prepared for was thoughtfulness or the undeniable charm he seemed to have in abundance.

"Okay, let's go," the director called.

Torrian turned to the camera with a wide smile. He picked up a spoon, and pounded it in the palm of his other hand. Paige read the words scrolling along the teleprompter with him.

"Paige Turner may have blasted my book, but I think it's time to find out who can really cook and who is just talk."

She hesitated just a second before reading, "Torrian Smallwood is a magician on the football field, but can the Fire Starter handle the heat in the kitchen, or will he get burned?"

"And cut," the director said.

Paige blinked twice. "That's it?"

"That's it," the director said. "It's only a ten-second spot. We'll have a voice-over doing an intro and exit."

"You mean we went through a half hour of makeup for two lines?"

"That's the way it works in television." Torrian shrugged.

"We want to get a couple of action shots of the both of you cooking," the director said. "Pretend as if you're bickering— but in a fun way. We'll roll the voice-over over these."

"Can you *pretend* to bicker with me?" Torrian asked, picking up a large stainless steel mixing bowl and cradling it against his side. His grin was sly and sexy and, for a moment, it put Paige in the same state of mindless shock she'd been in when the cameras first started to roll.

She was quick on the recovery, sending him a super sweet smile of her own as she slid a jar from the spice rack and added parsley flakes to the empty pot.

"Why should we pretend when the real thing is so much more convincing?" she asked.

Torrian threw his head back and laughed. It was so natural, so deep, so incredibly sexy. The picture of him on the cover of his cookbook popped into her mind, reminding Paige that behind that rich, seductive voice was a body to die for.

"Got it," the director called.

"You're both naturals," John said, coming from the side of the set.

"A natural in front of the camera. That's me," Paige snorted as she came from behind the cooking station.

A hand touched her elbow. "Hey, you did okay," Torrian said.

"Thank you," she said, trying to stave off the breathlessness that wanted to creep into her voice.

It was no use denying the healthy attraction snapping like firecrackers between them. Just the slightest touch from him caused her blood to boil. The longer that hand remained on her elbow, the shallower her breathing became, to the point that she was almost lightheaded by the time they made it back to the conference room.

"How did it go?" David asked when they reentered the conference room.

Torrian blew his question off with a wave of his hand. "I'm not the one who needs to worry," he said.

Paige cut her eyes at him, but could only laugh at his teasing gibe. "Did Jory and Peter leave?" she asked.

"Thank God," David nodded. "That's two of the biggest sports nuts I've ever met. They left me with a list of clients I now have to hit up for autographs."

"They are in heaven," Paige agreed.

"The station manager should be back in a minute to explain how the taping is going to work," David said. "Someone was typing out a schedule. They want to start with appetizers on Friday morning."

"Appetizers," Torrian mused. "You think you can handle that?"

Paige leveled him with a playfully stern look. "Bring. It. On."

Chapter 10

Torrian spotted Deirdre as soon as he walked through the swinging double doors that led to the Fire Starter Grille's state-of-the-art kitchen. He strolled up behind Dee and planted a kiss on her cheek. "I see your new toy finally arrived."

Deirdre whipped around. "Hey, there." She returned his kiss. "Yes, my toy is here." She smiled down at the gleaming professional-grade convection oven.

Torrian felt his eyes glazing over as Deirdre began an excited monologue about the wonders of the new oven. All he could think about was the woman he'd spent the morning with at the news station.

Paige Turner excited the hell out of him. It was as simple as that. But then, there was nothing simple about her. She was a contradiction wrapped up in a sinfully delicious package. One minute she was the confident, no-nonsense reviewer who had no qualms about standing up to him on her blog, and the next minute she was as timid as a schoolgirl, afraid of speaking in front of the camera.

As turned on as he'd been by that self-assured, I-can-do-anything attitude, witnessing her softer, more vulnerable side had ignited something in him that Torrian had yet to extinguish, even hours after leaving her at the TV station.

He'd felt that spark between them; had seen the look in her eyes as she'd held his gaze. She wasn't immune to this indescribable feeling that had taken hold of them since the moment they'd met, no matter how much she tried to fight it.

"Torrian!"

He jumped at Deirdre's fingers snapping in his face. "What?"

"I see you've been paying attention to every word I've said."

"Sorry, Dee. I've got a lot on my mind."

"That's what I was asking about. What was the big mysterious thing the people down at Channel 10 wanted to talk over with you and David?"

"They want me on their morning news show," Torrian answered.

"I figured that much," Deirdre said. She zeroed in on a smudge on the oven's door, rubbing it with the towel she pulled from her arm. "I just thought it was strange they wouldn't just come out and ask you over the phone, or through David. Why be so hush-hush about it?"

"I should clarify that," Torrian said. "They want me to *cook* on their morning show."

Deirdre's brow shot up. "You? Cook?"

"Hey," Torrian said. "I can get down in the kitchen when I have to."

"I know that. I'm the one who taught you. The problem is, you haven't had to 'get down' in the kitchen in years," Deirdre said, making air quotes with her fingers. "When was the last time you even scrambled your own egg?"

Torrian didn't waste time trying to remember. It had been years since he'd had to cook a meal for himself. If Deirdre didn't feed him, he had about a dozen five-star restaurants on speed dial. Not a single one of them offered delivery service, but Torrian always had a hot meal at his door within a half hour of his call.

"You're right," Torrian admitted. "Which is why I need you to give me a refresher course. If I'm going to win this competition, I've got to practice."

"Competition?"

"Paige Turner will be on the show, too." Torrian grinned at Dee's stunned look. "They've come up with this idea of a cook-off between me and Paige. Starting Friday, and for the next five weeks, we're going to prepare a dish on a special morning segment they're calling *Playing with Fire*. After each segment, a panel of judges will pick the better of the two dishes, and the station will give twenty-thousand dollars to a charity of the winner's choice. I picked Dante's high school band as one of my charities. I figure it'll help with their trip to Italy."

"Torrian, that's wonderful," Deirdre said. "But let's be honest, do you really think you have a chance of winning?"

"Have some faith, Dee." Torrian laughed. His sister leveled him with a sardonic look. Torrian held his hands up in surrender. "Okay, I'll admit it's been a while since I've had to cook for myself, but I'm not totally inept when it comes to the kitchen," Torrian said.

"I doubt it's enough to win in a competition, especially when you're going to be so distracted."

"What do you mean?"

Deirdre crossed her arms over her chest, a knowing look

on her face. "Don't even *try* to deny it. I know you've noticed how gorgeous Paige is."

"She's fine. So what?" Torrian shrugged. Deirdre wasn't buying it, which was expected. His sister was no fool. "Fine," Torrian exasperated. "She's gorgeous. Is that what you wanted me to say?"

"Yes," Deirdre smiled. "The first step is admitting your weakness, which for you, happens to be beautiful women."

"Are you going to help me out or what? Even though I think I can hold my own in the kitchen with Paige, a few pointers never hurt."

"When have I ever said no to you?" Deirdre asked, "Even when I probably should have."

"I knew I could count on you, Dee," he planted a kiss on her cheek. "I'm heading home. And instead of waiting for you to cook, I'm going to fend for myself tonight."

"Uh-huh," Deirdre murmured. "Remember to put those takeout boxes in the garbage."

Torrian's head fell back with a deep chuckle as he exited the kitchen.

Paige stared at the ceiling, too afraid to look at the clock on her nightstand. After her restless night getting out of bed was the last thing Paige wanted to do at the moment.

No. That was a lie.

The *last* thing she wanted to do was stand in front of that camera while all of New York watched her make a fool of herself. It wasn't just the thought of everyone in the tri-state area watching, but one person in particular, and he had the best seat in the house to witness her humiliation, seeing as he would be just steps away from her.

Paige expelled a frustrated sigh into the still air. She'd tried not to be so affected by him, but how could she not? The man was the object of millions of women's fantasies; how could she be immune?

Even if he had turned out to be a pretentious jerk, she would still have been physically attracted to him. But every day she discovered another reason why Torrian was the polar opposite of what she'd anticipated. Even when he brought up the blog, it was in a teasing, nonconfrontational way. He was no longer enemy number one. And that scared Paige more than anything.

"You can do this Olivia Paige."

She peered at the alarm clock. It was 4:29 a.m. She had to be at the studio in another hour and a half. She could sleep until five.

Paige turned over and covered her head with the other pillow.

"Oh, what*ever!*" she growled. There was no way she was falling back to sleep. She shoved the covers off, throwing her legs over the side of the bed.

"You were crazy to sign up for this in the first place."

Her cell phone rang, and Paige's heart instantly started to beat faster. A call this early in the morning was never good news. Before she'd even checked the caller ID, a dozen scenarios had run through her head. Had Dad's high blood pressure caught up with him and put him in the hospital with a stroke? Had something happened to one of her nieces or nephews?

Paige grabbed the phone from her bedside table and checked the tiny screen. She didn't recognize the number, but for some reason it seemed familiar.

"Hello?" she answered.

"Did I wake you?" came the low voice on the other end of the line.

Her heart rate escalated for an entirely new reason.

"It is four-thirty in the morning," Paige answered as

nonchalantly as she could while her brain raced with visions of how Torrian looked on the other side of the phone. What did he sleep in: pajamas or just boxers? She would not allow her mind to imagine him in nothing at all.

Paige pulled the phone away from her mouth so she could let out a quick, audible breath.

"I'm sorry," he was saying when she returned the phone to her ear. "I figured you would be awake since we have to be at the studio soon."

"Which begs the question, why are you calling when you're going to see me in just a few hours?"

"We never got the chance to finish the conversation we started over dinner," he answered. "I was hoping we could get our story straight before we got in front of the cameras today."

"So, what *is* our story?" Paige asked, scooting up and propping her back against the headboard.

"You tell me, Paige."

A tingle traveled down her spine at the sound of him saying her name. It was as soft as silk, and Paige could all too easily imagine that voice whispering in her ear in the early morning while he lay next to her in the flesh.

Get a grip! She had to get over this infatuation if she was going to work so closely with him.

"I told you, I won't lie to my readers," she said.

"I can respect that," he returned. "Just try to soften the blow, okay? I'm willing to say that I was riled up by your review and lost my temper. And your baiting me just fueled the fire."

"Did I really bait you?" she asked.

"C'mon, Paige." A hint of teasing lightened his voice. "You know those shots you took about last year's championship game were pretty cheap."

"I'll admit those were low blows, but I was only defending myself. Remember, you're the one who attacked first."

"Please stop using that word 'attack,'" he pleaded in a desperate whisper, his voice filled with remorse. "I don't attack women."

"I'm sorry," she returned softly, pulling the covers under her chin. At the pain she heard in his voice, all she wanted to do was make it better for him. "I'll go along with what you're suggesting," Paige said.

"Thank you." The words came out in a whoosh of soul-deep gratitude.

"It's the right thing to do," she continued. "I believe viewers will enjoy it more if we lighten the tone of the cook-off; make it a friendly competition. This should be more about our charities than about the rift between us."

"I don't like people thinking there is a rift between us." He paused, then said, "I don't like you thinking that either."

Paige tried to speak, but the words stuck in her throat. After a few difficult breaths she finally said, "I guess I can think of us as colleagues now that we're working together."

"You know I want more than that."

"I...Torrian," Paige started again. She wasn't sure what she wanted when it came to him. No, she knew what she wanted; she just didn't know if she could allow it.

"We have to be at the studio in a little over an hour," Torrian reminded her after she didn't speak for several moments.

"Oh, yes. Right," Paige said.

"Paige?"

"Yes?"

"Just because I'm a nice guy, don't think I won't clean the floor with you today. Be prepared to lose big." He chuckled, then disconnected.

Paige slammed the phone on the nightstand with more

force than necessary, determined to shut Torrian Smallwood's cocky, beautiful mouth.

Cooking might not be her favorite pastime, but she would never go hungry. It had been impossible for her not to pick up *some* culinary skills growing up in a family full of cooks. And with her sister Nicole's recipe for crawfish and crab crudités, Paige knew she had a killer recipe.

She quickly went through her normal morning routine, unwrapping the silk scarf she used to tie her hair down, and running a comb through it. The crew down at Channel 10 would take care of her makeup.

Throwing on her favorite running suit, Paige grabbed the bag she'd packed to bring with her to the studio.

When she walked outside, she decided to catch a cab instead of taking the subway. Fifteen minutes later, the driver pulled in front of the building that housed Channel 10. She took the elevator to the twenty-eighth floor and spotted Chelsea Robert through the glass doors.

"Good morning," the station manager greeted her. "I was just on my way to the green room to make sure everything was set up for you and Torrian."

Paige followed her to a room just off to the right of the conference room where they'd met earlier in the week.

"Help yourself to breakfast." Chelsea gestured to a variety of bagels arranged in a basket on a side table.

Paige eyed the food, and her stomach pitched. Her nerves were taking up all available space in there. "I probably shouldn't eat anything," Paige said, unable to disguise the slight tremble in her voice.

"You aren't nervous, are you?" Chelsea asked with a hint of concern.

"Not really," Paige lied. She opted for a bottle of water on her way to the seating area.

The look on Chelsea Robert's face said that she didn't believe Paige's claim, and Paige could not deny the spike of anxiety that had begun to thrum through her as the hour to her big television debut drew closer.

"I'm not used to being in front of a camera," she admitted. "So I guess I am a bit nervous. Don't worry, I'll be okay," she assured Chelsea.

"Oh, I know you will," she answered. "Just follow Torrian's lead. He's a natural."

Yes, he was. Paige had watched him in enough interviews over the years to know that Torrian was completely comfortable before the camera. Hopefully, once they got started, the edginess she was feeling would ease. Although having Torrian there wouldn't help; what he elicited in her was far from calming.

The door opened and John, the production assistant who'd guided them to makeup the first day they'd come to the studio, entered, followed by Torrian who looked so good he didn't need to worry about going to hair and makeup.

"Good morning," Torrian greeted in his deep voice.

"Good morning," Paige and Chelsea answered at the same time.

Chelsea clamped her hands together. "Well, now that you're both here, I'm going to turn this over to John. He'll take you up to makeup in just a bit, but first, he's going to cover a few details," Chelsea finished. She left with a promise to see them both just before the first segment.

After Torrian declined John's offer of coffee, the production assistant said, "Okay, then." He opened his mouth again, then closed it. A pained expression creased his forehead. "I forgot my notes," he grimaced. "I'll be back in just a sec."

Torrian walked over to the sofa and took a seat. "So,

how has your morning been so far? Other than having some annoying pest wake you at four in the morning?"

"It's been okay, other than that pest." She grinned. She gestured to the cream-colored cashmere sweater that molded to his sculpted chest. "You're not cooking in that are you?"

He looked down at himself. "I was planning to."

"That's just showing off," Paige scoffed.

A huge grin spread across his face, displaying his perfect white teeth, and causing a spike in her heart rate.

"I'll wear an apron if it'll make you feel better."

"Thanks," she snorted. She ran a shaking hand along the hair at her nape, the anxiousness fueling her adrenaline to the point that she was ready to jump out of her seat. She had to get a hold of herself.

"Are you still nervous?" Torrian asked.

She glanced over at him and admitted, "Yes. I can't help it. I'm afraid I'll freeze as soon as those cameras start to roll." Paige turned to him. "Please don't let me make a fool of myself," she pleaded. "If I look like a deer caught in headlights, just start talking."

"I don't get it. Where's all that confidence that comes through on your blog?"

"That's different."

"You can hide behind your computer." His voice was filled with understanding.

"Yes," she admitted. "The blog and my column are the perfect medium to be heard and not seen. I've always had a fear of speaking in public." Because she always messed up.

"You have nothing to fear." Torrian reached between them and took her hand. He ran his fingers over her skin. "Once we start, you'll forget those cameras are even there."

She doubted it, but the low timbre of his voice lulled her into almost believing there was some truth to his words. Delicious warmth radiated from where his fingers touched her.

"But if I don't, you'll make sure I don't look like an idiot, right?"

"You couldn't look like an idiot if you tried," Torrian said, his voice still low, not quite seductive but definitely in the neighborhood.

John came back into the green room. He held up a clipboard. "I'm still learning," he apologized. "We're going to open up with a five-and-a-half-minute interview with the both of you on the main set. We'll go into the background of the blog controversy, and what makes you two such great adversaries."

"Actually," Torrian said, "Paige and I discussed this, and we'd rather not be seen as adversaries."

"But that's the whole point of the cook-off," John said, clearly deflated.

"It's what gave you all the *idea* for the cook-off," Torrian reminded him. "We'd rather make this more about the charities than the little thing that happened on her blog."

"I know that, but—"

Torrian shook his head. Paige recognized that conciliatory smile. She'd seen him use it on reporters who tried to pry personal information out of him during interviews. John was going to get about as far as those interviewers got, which wasn't very far at all.

"Look," Torrian said, "New Yorkers know what to expect from Torrian Smallwood, and it's not some guy who spars with a woman, especially one as beautiful as Paige." The smile he sent her was more genuine, and caused Paige's breath to hitch. He was laying on the charm, but Paige had a feeling it was no longer just for John's benefit. "We want to make it clear that there's no more bad blood lingering because of her blog. And whatever bantering we do on camera will be good-natured fun. Right, Paige?"

"Yes." Paige nodded.

"Don't worry; your viewers will still be entertained," Torrian assured him.

"I should give the anchor a heads-up, just in case some questions need to be adjusted," John said, heading back out the door.

Paige crossed her arms over her chest and shook her head. "How did you manipulate that entire situation right before my eyes?"

"They're going to get their ratings no matter what," Torrian answered. "But it won't be at the expense of either of our reputations."

He said it as if they were a team; the two of them against the big bad media.

"So, is that what we're striving for, good-natured bantering?"

He smiled that smile again; the one where the corner of his mouth lifted up just a bit. It made something tremble at the base of her stomach. "I think we've moved past the bickering stage, don't you?"

"There are stages at play here?"

"Yes." He nodded. He leaned an inch closer. Then another. "There are those milestones two people encounter as they fight the attraction building between them. Just to be clear, I'm no longer fighting it, but since you are, I'll lay them out for you.

"First, they try to fight it." He leaned closer. "Then they think if they just forget about it, it'll all go away. Finally, they acknowledge it. One may still shy away, but it becomes pretty clear that there's no use. The attraction between us is even more intense, so I doubt it'll take long to reach the ultimate goal."

His decadent voice had reached a new level of seduction.

"Why are you doing this?" Paige asked, though she already knew the answer. She'd known it from the minute their eyes connected. The attraction between them was tangible, a thick, cloaking presence that drugged her senses. Paige realized stage fright should be the least of her worries—being pulled in by the desire in Torrian's eyes was much more deadly.

"Stop thinking so hard," he said. He took her chin in his hand and lowered his mouth to hers.

The instant his soft, sensual mouth touched hers Paige's entire body ignited. Slowly, decadently, he brushed his lips back and forth, teasing her senses and feeding the desire that had been building within her for days. His kiss was delicate, but it quickly became dangerous when he angled his head and urged her lips to part. As soon as they did, Torrian's tongue pushed its way into her mouth.

His tongue stroked in a wickedly insistent rhythm, thrusting against her own and reminding Paige of everything that had been missing in her life for so very long. The feeble protest her brain tried to conjure was no match for the assault being waged against her senses with such carnal skill. As his tongue dipped in and out, Paige couldn't help the erotic images that flashed through her mind. Images of her body draped over Torrian's as their erotic kiss led to something more.

With a reluctance that came through loud and clear with his groan, he pulled away. Paige felt his warm breath on her face as he whispered, "We'll talk about this later."

Her eyes flew open, but before she had a chance to form a coherent thought, John came back through the door. "Makeup is ready," he said.

Paige forced herself to shake off the remnants of their kiss as she tried to focus her mind on the interview that was about to take place. It felt as if the knots in her stomach were twisting and tying, turning her insides into a tangled mess.

Had Torrian done that just to rattle her? No, he probably thought his kiss would help to lessen her distress about being in front of the camera. But he was wrong, and Paige had a feeling her nervousness over the interview would pale in comparison to the new anxiety Torrian's sensual kiss had created within her.

Chapter 11

Torrian cocked one leg atop the opposite knee and stretched his arm across the back of the loveseat. If she questioned him later, he would tell Paige he adopted the pose because he wanted to foster a feeling of relaxed camaraderie between them.

In all honesty, he just wanted to touch her.

He'd been bowled over by the vulnerability he'd witnessed when she pleaded with him to take over if she got stage fright. He wanted to wipe that fear from her eyes; to protect her.

He looked over and noted Paige's stiff, set jaw. He squeezed her shoulder. "Relax," he said. "Take a deep breath. Remember, it's like you're having a conversation with a few people."

"And half of New York," Paige said.

"Forget the cameras," Torrian reiterated. "Pretend they're not even here. Look at this." He motioned to the set. "It's like we're in a living room talking with friends."

Paige sucked in a lungful of air and let it out with a whoosh.

"Okay," she said with a self-assured nod of her head. "Wow, I actually feel…better."

"You have to learn to trust me," he said, giving her shoulder another squeeze. She had yet to knock his hand away, one notch in the plus column.

The news anchor came running toward them, one of the hairdressers close on her heels. She sat in the comfy armchair and asked, "Are we ready?"

Paige flung his hand from her shoulder and shifted a few inches away from him. He bit back a smile.

"We are now," Torrian answered.

The hairdresser sprayed the anchor's hair, flipped a curl, and dashed out of the way.

"Here we go," the anchor said, then immediately turned to the camera straight ahead. "Welcome back. This morning, we have a real treat for our viewers. The juiciest gossip to hit New York in the last few weeks has been the online war between popular entertainment columnist, Paige Turner, and Sabers wide receiver, Torrian Smallwood. The two have decided to bring their battle into our studios here at Channel 10."

The anchor finished her introduction, then turned to Paige and Torrian.

"We've all read the review that started all of this, Paige. What was it about Torrian's book that you hated so much?"

Torrian sensed her stiffen but then relax. "Actually, Stephenie, I think people have blown this entire situation out of proportion. I didn't hate Torrian's book per se. Did I have a few issues with it? Sure. But hate it?" Paige shook her head.

Torrian had not realized his muscles had tensed so much until he let out a breath, and the tension with it.

Paige continued. "I think this is another case of me writing what I thought was a funny, tongue-in-cheek review, only to find that my words were taken completely out of context."

"I think that's happened to all of us a time or two," the

anchor replied. She turned her attention to him. "Unfortunately for you, Torrian, when it happens to a well-known celebrity, the ripple effects last much longer."

"Yes, they do," Torrian answered. "I guess I have a bit of learning to do. I think there's still hope for me, if Paige is willing to help."

She actually blushed. It was gorgeous on her.

"Well, all of New York is still buzzing about your online skirmish, and we're all anxious to see who comes out on top in your battle in the kitchen."

"I have my own prediction," Torrian answered, "but there's only one way to find out."

The anchor looked into the camera. "Thankfully, for us, New York, the wait is almost over. Stay tuned for round one of *Playing with Fire*."

The anchor took out her ear piece. "That was good," she said. "I was a bit concerned when John said we wouldn't be working the sworn-enemies angle, but I think viewers will like this more. Good luck in the kitchen today," she said.

John left his post next to the cameraman. "The kitchen is almost ready," he said. "You'll both need to be there in the next five minutes."

Paige pushed up from the sofa, and Torrian quickly followed her. "That was painless, wasn't it?" he asked.

"Almost." She laughed. "I hate to admit it, but you were right. I probably would have been a lot less comfortable if we were duking it out during that interview. Things flowed a lot better without the fighting."

"The one thing I don't want to do with you is fight," Torrian said.

He stared down at her and allowed the desire that had been building within him to show in his eyes. He wanted to make sure there was no mistaking what he had in mind.

He wanted her.

She held his gaze, her lips slightly parted, understanding, naked and raw, in her eyes.

"You don't take no for an answer, do you?" she panted.

"What do you think?" Torrian asked.

John came up to them. "We're ready to start." He ushered them toward the kitchen.

When Torrian arrived at his cooking station, the ingredients for his crepes were portioned in a half dozen small stainless steel bowls and arranged around the cook top. They had been told beforehand that they could cook the food that would be judged off-air, but Deirdre had warned that the crepes would be rubbery if he made them ahead of time. The filling was ready, and the plates were decorated with curly green garnish, but to secure a win, Torrian would have to get the crepes done during their cooking segment.

Paige took her place behind her stove. She seemed to have recovered from the moment that had passed between them. She picked up the blue-and-white pin-striped apron with the KWEZ Channel 10 logo etched into the center and pulled it over her head, tying it in the back.

She looked over at him and expelled a dramatic sigh. "Please put that apron on."

Torrian's head flew back with a crack of laughter. He tied his apron around his waist. "Are you still not going to tell me what you're cooking?"

"Nope," she said. "You'll find out when the rest of New York does."

"It had better be good," he warned. "I predict my dish is going to be the most popular appetizer on the menu at my restaurant."

"Well, *I* predict you'll be asking me for my recipe once we're done today," she said with an extra sweet smile.

Torrian returned the smile. "We'll see about that."

* * *

Paige didn't know what happened, but as soon as the camera started rolling every bit of anxiety she'd been feeling vanished. The light banter Torrian had promised occurred naturally between them.

The camera was focused on him at the moment. He spoke to the audience with a presence that commanded attention.

"The key when making crepes is to make sure you spread the batter evenly," Torrian said as he used the bottom of the ladle to smooth the thin batter. "You have to keep your eyes on them because they'll burn in an instant."

He flipped the crepe over, and Paige couldn't help but be impressed by its perfect coloring.

"Spoon about three teaspoons of the spinach and artichoke mixture into the center of each crepe and fold the sides over." He folded the paper-thin pancakes. "I see you drooling over there," he said, looking up from his task long enough to send Paige a sly, impossibly sexy grin. "Don't worry, there's enough for you."

"They do look pretty," Paige said, "Unfortunately for you, I believe our judges have taste buds."

"Ouch." He put a hand to his chest. "You mind keeping your daggers on your side of the kitchen?"

"Sorry, but the truth does hurt," Paige answered with exaggerated sorrow.

"Just for the record, I added a little crow to your crepe. I have a feeling you'll be eating some pretty soon."

"Good one." Paige pointed her finger at him. "Gotta love your confidence." She shrugged nonchalantly as she added garnish to her dish. "Of course, confidence is about the only thing you have going for you, because those crepes won't get you very far."

"Can someone please get the knives away from her?" he called out, his eyes roaming around the studio as if searching for someone to come to his aid. There was a flurry of laughter around the set.

The camera cut back to the news desk. The morning anchor, who was still grinning, said, "We'll see who our celebrity judges choose as the first-round winner in this most spirited kitchen battle."

Torrian walked over to her, a smile pulling at the corner of his mouth. "You got over that camera shyness pretty quickly."

"I did," Paige agreed. "This has been more fun than I thought it would be."

"The cooking or the cheap shots you keep taking at me?"

"Oh, definitely the cheap shots." She chuckled. She leaned toward him. "I'll let you in on a little secret. I hate to cook."

"It's a good thing I'm available as your target. This would be torture if you had no one to grill."

"It's nothing personal." Paige continued to grin. "You *are* being a good sport about all of this. Just let me know if I go too far."

"You'd have to get a lot nastier to reach too-far status," Torrian answered. "Compared to what I have to put up with from reporters, you're being downright friendly."

"You do shoulder a lot of criticism, don't you?" The realization caused Paige to feel a twinge of regret for some of the things she'd said to him.

Torrian shrugged it off. "It comes with the territory. I guess I didn't realize it would be more of the same with the book and restaurant. Maybe I should be thanking you. Now I know what's to come from other food and book critics."

"Not necessarily," Paige said. She couldn't keep the wry smile from surfacing. "After all the heat you've taken over my review, I'm sure all the other critics will take it easy on you."

"You may be right." He paused, then continued. "I'm happy you decided to do the show. We have a natural rapport once those cameras start to roll."

"That seems to be the case," Paige agreed, her eyes locked with his. She felt herself staring, but even when she tried to pull away, her brain wouldn't let her. "I think viewers will respond to this better than they would have responded to a formal apology. We're actually *showing* them that there are no hard feelings between us."

"So, there are none?"

"Hard feelings? I thought we already took care of that."

"I still wasn't sure," Torrian said. He stepped closer, leaned in, and with a whisper, said, "Maybe if you actually accepted a dinner invitation from me, it would convince me."

Paige stopped short. A rush of heat flowed over her skin at the hushed, sensual tone in his voice.

"C'mon, Paige?" he continued, his warm, moist breath like a tantalizing wisp of sensation in her ear. "It's not as if we haven't gone out to dinner before."

"That was by accident," she said, infinitely grateful her voice did not crack. "And I told you then that there could be nothing between us."

"I didn't like your reason."

Paige forced herself to break out from under the sensual web his nearness had woven around her. She knew what was at stake if she allowed herself to be seen with Torrian in anything other than a professional light. If she landed that syndication deal, people would automatically think she'd used his celebrity to make it happen.

"What's the real reason you won't go out with me?" Torrian asked.

Paige stepped away from him, needing the physical distance to clear her head. "I don't owe you an explanation," she said.

"This is just the way it is; the way it has to be. I hope you can accept that."

"What if I can't?"

The urgency in his voice caused Paige's head to whip around. She found nothing but raw honesty in his hazel eyes.

He glanced over to the stagehand who was setting up the table where the three judges would judge their recipes in the next segment. Torrian grabbed her elbow and gently tugged her toward the back of the set.

"Paige, I haven't been able to think about anything but you for days," he admitted. "It doesn't matter where I am or what I'm doing. You can't expect me to ignore this."

Paige closed her eyes and took a long, deep breath. Need burned deep within her chest. A part of her wanted to say to hell with professionalism. So what if everyone thought she'd only glommed on to Torrian because of his celebrity? She knew differently. Why deny them both the chance to explore the heat that had erupted between them simply because she was afraid of what others would say?

Paige looked up at him. The intensity in his stare stole her breath.

Just say yes, her mind pleaded. Hadn't she done enough to prove that she could make it on her own? She was tired of living her life for what others thought.

With a leap of faith as long as the skies were vast, Paige grabbed hold of Torrian's gaze and said simply, "Okay."

His eyes widened at her answer, as if he didn't believe it.

"If you're willing to keep it a secret," she continued. Even though she'd just told herself that what others thought didn't matter, she was not going to give them something to talk about if she didn't have to. "I'm willing to see where this… this attraction between us will lead. Just promise me we'll be discreet."

A slow smile curled at the edge of his mouth. "I can do discreet," he said. "Can I see you tonight? I can come to your place; cook you dinner. I'll dress in baggy sweats and a baseball cap. No one will ever know it's me."

Paige let out a tired laugh. "This is crazy."

He shrugged. "I agree. But if this is how you want it, it's what I have to do. I'm willing to do whatever it takes."

He was. Resolve shone through his eyes.

"We're almost ready for the judging segment," one of the associate producers called.

Torrian squeezed her arm, drawing her attention back to him. "What do you say, Paige?"

She shoved away the lingering doubts and decided to take a chance on fate.

"I'll see you tonight."

Chapter 12

Torrian parked his BMW two blocks from Paige's brownstone. He was taking no chances. He understood her need for discretion, even if he didn't share it. Over the past seven years, he'd become immune to the media's scrutiny of his love life.

According to the papers, his latest girlfriend was a woman who had been in front of him while he was in line to buy a bagel. A photographer from *The Post* happened to be in the vicinity, and that was apparently all that was needed to make it the gospel truth. It had been a stretch for *The Post* to convince the public his make-believe relationship with Bagel Woman was front-page news, but having him linked romantically with Paige…People would eat it up.

Torrian wasn't ready to share; he wanted her all to himself.

He quickly made his way up the steps and pressed the button next to Paige's name.

"Torrian?" she asked.

"Not a good way to answer your doorbell. What if it wasn't me?"

"Sorry, I'm not used to subterfuge," she answered. "Come on up." A buzzer sounded, followed by a click. Torrian transferred the bag of groceries to his left hand and pulled open the heavy door. He took the steps up to her third-floor apartment two at a time. When he arrived on her landing, Paige was waiting just inside her door.

"Hi," she greeted, opening the door so he could slip in, then quickly closing it behind him.

"Good evening," Torrian answered.

Damn, he wanted to kiss her. For a second, Torrian saw himself dropping the groceries in the middle of the room and snatching her face between his hands. Instead, he walked over to her kitchen and deposited the grocery bag on the counter, then turned to face Paige.

She was dressed in a slim skirt and a form-fitting shirt that clung to her perfectly sized breasts. She wasn't big by any stretch of the imagination, but her breasts were the perfect size for her frame. Torrian had become disenchanted with disproportionate, gargantuan chests years ago. He much preferred the look and feel of a natural woman.

"For a minute I wasn't sure you would answer the door."

"Why wouldn't I?" Paige asked.

"I thought maybe you were still upset about me winning the first competition."

Her eyes narrowed with disapproval, but there was a hint of amusement around the edges. "Enjoy it while you can. It'll be the last win you get." She grinned. "What's in the bag?" Paige nodded toward the sack he held.

"Stuff," he answered.

"You truly have to stop being so forthcoming," she snorted.

He loved that sound from her. From any other woman it would be unladylike, but with Paige, it was charming.

"I convinced Deirdre to give me one of her best recipes, but it's top secret."

Paige frowned. "I was going to help you cook."

Torrian shook his head. "I have kitchen duty tonight, and if we're going to eat at a decent hour, I need to get started."

She crossed her arms, a grin curving the corner of her mouth in the sexiest way. "You know, this is the first time I've had a man cook me dinner," Paige admitted.

"Good. That means there's no one for you to compare me to," Torrian laughed. "I'll need a small saucepan and a skillet."

She retrieved his request from a bottom cabinet. "Are you sure I can't help you with anything?" she asked.

Torrian looked over at her; the urge to attack her mouth with his tongue was stronger than ever. He sucked in a long, deep breath, begging for control. Instead of the request that first popped in his mind, Torrian said, "If you don't mind, I could use a glass of wine."

"Fine." She shrugged. "If that's the way you want it."

If he could really have what he wanted, he'd throw the groceries to the side, take her in his arms and spend the rest of the night exploring her luscious mouth, the curve of her waist, the hollow behind her knee and all parts in between.

"White or red," Paige asked, her head in the refrigerator.

Her rounded butt poked out, and it was all he could do not to run up behind her and fill his hands with it. Torrian gripped the edge of the counter, searching for control. He would go crazy if he had to spend the rest of the night in this state of arousal.

"Red for me to drink and white for the sauce," he answered.

Unpacking the groceries, he withdrew chicken, extra-virgin olive oil, chives, lemons, wild rice and a small vial of white truffle oil that Deirdre had told him to guard with his life.

"Hmm…a piece of the secret is revealed," Paige grinned, walking over to him with a bottle in each hand. Damn, she looked good with that playful smile on her lips.

"I've got to watch myself around you," Torrian teased, unwrapping the chicken cutlets from the white butcher paper. "You make it too easy for me to let my guard down."

"I could say the same about you." She handed him a glass of ruby-colored wine. "It's not every day that I allow a man into my kitchen," she said. "And to be honest, up until the moment you rang the doorbell, I was debating whether to call it off."

"Why didn't you?" he asked

She hid behind her wineglass, taking two short sips. She slowly lowered the glass to the counter and pushed herself up and onto it, crossing her legs. "Because I wanted to see you. I wanted you in my kitchen, cooking me dinner." She paused, the span of time so long that Torrian thought she wasn't going to speak again. She looked away, then back at him, a mixture of apprehension and frank honesty in her eyes. "I wanted to spend time with you, Torrian."

Her softly spoken words made the decision for him.

He strolled to where Paige was perched on the counter. He put his hands on either side of her, and seeing permission in her eyes, leaned in close and captured her lips in a slow, gentle kiss.

Nothing had ever tasted this good.

She was soft and sweet and more delicious than the most decadent dessert. Torrian tested his tongue against her lips, begging them to open, aching inside when they didn't. He crept along the invisible line of propriety, cautious of going too far too soon. He wouldn't take more than she was willing to give.

He tried to pull away, but Paige's moan reined him back into the kiss. She parted her lips, whether as an invitation or just for air, Torrian didn't know, but he used the opportunity to fully explore all her kiss had to offer. He forged ahead with his tongue, running it along her smooth teeth and pushing farther into the sensual warmth of her mouth. She tasted like coffee and chocolate. Sweet and addictive, a drug to his brain.

Another moan came from deep in her throat, and the sexy sound sent a stalk of electricity straight to his groin. Torrian fisted one hand in her short hair, holding her head to his. He ran the other hand up and down her back, along her side, down to the gentle curve of her waist and the flair of her hip.

His arousal strained against his fly. He was dying to push Paige's tight skirt up to her waist so her legs could open for him. He was desperate to touch her. He wanted to experience the moist, hot feel of her core against his fingers.

The hiss of sizzling oil forced Torrian out of the sensual hold. He disengaged from the kiss that would have gone on for hours in a perfect world.

"Damn," he whispered as he stepped back, his body instantly mourning the loss of her nearness. If the hazy look in her eyes was any indication, she had been just as affected by their kiss. Her lips were opened slightly, calling him in for another round, but the stench of burning oil forced his attention to the stove.

Torrian removed the pan, emptying the dark, caramel-colored oil down the drain.

He looked over at Paige. Her eyes still held that slightly dazed look, but she'd recovered enough to take another sip from her wineglass.

"Are you going to say anything?" he asked.

She paused with the glass halfway to her mouth, looked away, then looked back at him and shook her head. She drained the glass.

Torrian ran cold water over the skillet, a plume of white smoke escaping into the air. "You have to say something," he told her. He returned the skillet to the stove and coated the bottom with more olive oil, his hand shaking slightly, the effects of that kiss still coursing through his bloodstream. "Otherwise, how am I supposed to know if I'm allowed to do it again?"

"You're allowed," she answered immediately.

Torrian looked up at her and couldn't help the grin that curled the edge of his lips. "Good," he answered, "Because I'm not sure I would have been able to help myself."

"It's probably best you don't until after dinner is finished, though," Paige said. "You have a history of setting kitchens on fire, and I don't want mine to become one of your victims."

"The lady has jokes."

"Occasionally," Paige said. She scooted from her perch on the countertop. "And, since I don't want to be any more of a distraction, I'll go and set the table."

"Dinner won't take very long," Torrian promised.

As she was exiting the kitchen, Torrian caught her arm and pulled her to him for what was supposed to be a swift kiss, but when he tried to pull away, Paige went with him. She wrapped an arm around his neck and leaned into him, her breasts cushioning his chest.

The oil sizzled.

He backed away, heaving a huge breath. "Okay, we've got to stop that. I can't afford to ruin any more olive oil. Then again…" Torrian said, noting the husky look in her eyes. "What's a little burnt oil?"

He leaned in for another kiss, but Paige stopped him.

"No." She laughed. "I can wait until after dinner."

He wasn't sure if he could. One thing he knew for sure, he didn't want to stop at just a kiss. He wanted much, *much* more.

But did she?

"What's going to happen after dinner, Paige?" The look that came over her face told Torrian he should have stopped while he was ahead. "I'm sorry," he said. "Forget I asked that."

"It's something we'll have to discuss sooner or later," Paige said.

"We can discuss it later," Torrian answered. "I don't want you to think I'm pressuring you into anything."

"I won't let you pressure me into anything I don't want to do," she returned. "When it happens, it will be a mutual decision."

Not if, but *when*.

His gut clenched. The erection he'd tried desperately to curb swelled even more at the promise he witnessed in Paige's gaze.

God, he wanted her. Torrian had to clench his fist against the urge to capture her mouth again and satisfy the desire that had them both taking deep, labored breaths.

"Go set the table," he said.

Paige nodded.

His skin still on fire after their kiss, Torrian followed Deirdre's written instructions without fully processing what he was doing. His mind continued to conjure the way Paige's lips felt against his—soft, pliable. Like heaven.

"Are you sure you don't need any help?"

His head whipped around sharply, finding Paige at the edge of the kitchen. The look on her face was tentative; as if she was unsure she should even approach. It was probably best she didn't, not if they wanted to eat.

"I'm almost done," he told her. "Why don't you pour the wine? I'll be in there in a few minutes."

Torrian fluffed the wild rice with a fork. He heaped several spoonfuls onto each plate, then covered the rice with a sautéed chicken breast, drizzling truffle oil along the perimeter of the dish. He carried a plate in each hand to the small dining area. Paige sat at the table in the corner of her apartment. She'd set the table with place mats, silverware and a single votive candle in the center. The wine chilled in a ceramic bowl filled with ice.

"Sorry I don't have a wine bucket. I'm not used to entertaining," she said with a delicate shrug.

"It's perfect," Torrian assured her. They could have been on the floor, with nothing but their hands to eat with and it would have still been perfect, as long as she was sitting across from him.

"This looks amazing," Paige commented as he set a plate before her. She inhaled and sighed. "Smells amazing, too," she said, slight dejection in her voice.

"You say that as if it's a bad thing," Torrian said.

"It is. I'm in competition with you, remember?" she said, her mouth tipping up in a smile.

Torrian drank in that smile. It was lovely, just like the rest of her. "Don't worry," he said. "I promise to throw one of the contests so you can win."

"Thanks," she snorted. "So." She held up her wineglass. "Should we toast?"

"To what?" he asked.

She tipped her head to the side. "I'm not sure."

"I can think of a thing or two," Torrian answered. He instinctively leaned closer. "Like that fact that we've discovered something better to do than fight."

"What's that?" Paige asked, leaning closer.

"This." He captured her mouth in another kiss. It was swift

and sweet and didn't last nearly as long as he would have liked. He sat back in the chair. "We need to get to eating so we can finish this meal," he said.

Settling back in her chair, Paige inhaled. "It really does smell delicious. Your sister must be an awesome chef."

"She is," Torrian answered. "She earns her certification in a few weeks."

"From what I read in your book, she's the reason you're where you are today."

"I owe everything to Deirdre," Torrian admitted. "I probably would have been your everyday statistic, dead or in jail, if not for her."

"She must be so proud of what you've become."

He nodded. "I'm just sorry I couldn't get us to the Super Bowl last year. I always told Deirdre I would give her my first Super Bowl ring."

"I'm not talking about you as a football player. I'm more impressed with Torrian Smallwood, the man."

"You are?" His brow rose. "What is it about Torrian, the man, that impresses you?"

She stabbed a small piece of chicken with her fork, using the sliver of meat to pick up a bit of the truffle oil. "You're a great role model for kids. Unlike a lot of pro ball players, you seem to consider the consequences of your actions off the field. And despite that one slip up on my blog, you really are a gentleman."

"Thank you," Torrian said. If he could take back what had happened on her blog, he would in a heartbeat. "I'm sorry about the blog," he apologized yet again.

"Stop beating yourself up about that, Torrian. Look at all the good that's come out of it. We wouldn't be sitting here right now if you hadn't responded to my review."

He took her hand in his and brought her fingers to his

lips. "You're right," he said. "It'll still be a long time before I forgive myself, though."

"Why don't you try, just for tonight," Paige said. "I don't want to talk about the fighting that brought us here."

"Neither do I," Torrian answered. "What I really want to know is why someone with your fear of public speaking would agree to do the show?"

There was a crafty glint in her eyes. "I knew you would bring that up again."

He shrugged. "I just figured you must have a good reason."

She dabbed the corners of her mouth. "This is still just speculation, but my weekly column is up for syndication in several national magazines."

"But your column is specific to stuff going on in New York, isn't it?"

"Yes, but it would fit well in dozens of travel and leisure magazines, including airline magazines. It's a huge market."

"Never thought about that," Torrian nodded.

"My first instinct was to refuse KWEZ, but when Jory told me about the potential syndication deal, we both decided it was best I get as much exposure as possible."

"So, what do you have to do in order to get syndicated?"

"It varies with different publications. In my case, it's a huge magazine conglomerate that is in charge of several travel and leisure magazines. Want to know the most ironic thing? Their corporate headquarters are in the same building as KWEZ."

"It's fate," Torrian said, wiping his mouth with the napkin.

"Or the quickest way for me to completely mess this up for myself," Paige said.

"Don't think that way. If I were you, I'd stop in at the

magazine and introduce myself to the head guy. Be aggressive about it."

"I'd rather stand naked in the middle of Central Park."

Torrian's stomach automatically tightened at the image that popped into his mind. He had to bite back the words that nearly slipped out of his mouth.

"Now, if I were to casually run into Stephen Cambridge in the elevator…" Paige continued.

Torrian's eyes widened. "Wait, who did you say?"

"Stephen Cambridge. He's the CEO of the Cambridge Group."

Torrian let the smile develop slowly on his face.

"What?" Paige asked.

"My beach house in the Hamptons is three doors down from his," Torrian said. "What would you give to meet him?"

"Oh, you play dirty."

"Is it working?"

She caught her bottom lip between her teeth and nodded. Torrian pushed away from the table and went to her, pulling her up from the chair. She wrapped her arms around his neck and tilted her head back, in perfect position for his mouth to capture hers in a slow, mind-drugging kiss.

It was several minutes later before they came up for air. Torrian's entire body was on fire, and the arousal pressing into her stomach left nothing to the imagination. God, he would give anything to have her take him by the hand and lead him to her bedroom. His body hardened more just at the thought.

As if she'd read his mind, Paige pulled back.

"Thank you for dinner," she said. "If the food at your restaurant is even half this good, you have nothing to worry about."

"It'll be twice this good," Torrian managed to say. In reality, he couldn't recall a single thing about the meal they'd shared just minutes ago. His entire being was consumed by the need to join his body with hers.

Expectation ignited in the air, sending a surge of anticipation shooting through his bloodstream.

"It's getting late," Paige said, her words dousing the fire more effectively than a bucket of ice water.

Torrian's shoulders sagged, his slim hope for a night of sweat-filled lovemaking dying a swift death. It would happen. Maybe not tonight, but soon. The passion building between them was too strong to ignore.

"I'll help you clean up," he said.

"No." Paige shook her head. "You cooked. I've got cleanup duty."

"Are you sure?" he asked, still holding on to her. He wasn't a fan of scrubbing pans, but he'd do anything to stay with her a little longer.

"I've got it." Paige nodded, disengaging from his hold. She picked up their plates and headed for the kitchen.

Torrian sucked in a lungful of air in an attempt to calm the raging need still racing at lightning speed throughout his body. It would kill him to leave her tonight. He knew he was moving too fast, expecting her to sleep with him when just two weeks ago they were at each other's throats.

But he wanted her. The need was so strong it nearly brought him to his knees.

Torrian leaned over and blew out the votive candle. He plucked the wineglasses from the table and placed them on the bar that separated the kitchen from the living room. Paige came around the edge of the galley kitchen. She stared at him, her eyes pulling him in like twin magnets. Torrian wasn't sure how much time had passed between them.

"Can I see you tomorrow?" Paige finally asked.

"Yes," Torrian answered immediately. She could see him

every day for the rest of his life. "Do you want me to come over for dinner again?"

"Sure," Paige answered, taking his hand and angling to the door.

Dinner was another twenty-two hours away. His entire body mourned at the thought of not seeing her for such an extended period of time.

"Can we make it breakfast instead?" Torrian asked. "I don't want to wait until tomorrow night to see you."

A soft smile graced her lips. "Me neither," she said. Paige nodded toward his arm. "Can you exercise with your injury?" she asked.

"A bit."

"Then how about a run in Central Park? It's another good way to go incognito. I know a quiet, out-of-the-way place in the park where we can have breakfast when we're done."

He pinned her to the door and leaned in close. "What time should I meet you?" he asked, his lips only a breath away from hers.

"Six too early for you?"

"Not at all," he answered.

"Meet me at the 86th Street entrance," Paige said. "I'll have on a pink-and-green running suit."

"I can't wait to see you in it," he said, unable to stop himself from capturing her lips in one last kiss that left them both breathless.

When he finally let her up for air, Paige put her hand to her chest. "What will you be wearing?" she asked, still breathing hard.

Torrian put on the baseball cap he'd arrived with and pulled it low on his head. "This cap, a pair of sunglasses and a huge smile the minute I see you." He opened the door and gave her another swift kiss. "See you tomorrow."

* * *

Paige stood just inside the gate at the 86th Street entrance to Central Park. She bent her right leg back and caught her ankle in her hand, giving her right quad a nice, long stretch.

"Torrian, where are you?" Paige said under her breath. He was only ten minutes late, but still, there was only so much stretching she could do to keep her muscles warm.

"Good morning."

Paige jumped and turned. Torrian stood right behind her, wearing the baseball cap from last night, sunshades, loose-fitting running shorts and a T-shirt.

"You're late," Paige said. She stifled the urge to kiss him, then decided what the hell; he was incognito. She planted a quick kiss on his lips.

"First time I ever got rewarded for being late," Torrian said.

"That was *my* reward for waiting so patiently for you," she answered. "Come on, time to run."

Paige took off along the running path on the massive park's east side. She and Torrian settled into an easy, twelve-minute-mile pace, just fast enough to get the blood pumping through her veins. They turned left and jogged past the Metropolitan Museum of Art, then crossed East Drive just before the obelisk.

"Why don't we cut across so we can run along the lake?" Paige suggested.

"And get off the path?" Torrian asked.

"There's nothing that says we have to run along the path," she said, and sprinted across the grass.

"You don't play around, do you?" Torrian said, catching up to her after about a minute of lagging behind.

"Next month I start training for my eighth marathon."

He groaned. "You should have told me that before I agreed to run with you."

"You're an athlete. I didn't think I'd have to take it easy on you," Paige answered.

"There's a big difference between the kind of PT we do for football and distance running."

"Just let me know if you get tired," Paige said. She was tempted to up her pace, but only because it was such an amazing morning.

They jogged along the edge of Belvedere Lake, toward the center of Central Park. The Great Lawn just north of the lake was already peppered with people getting an early start to their morning.

"Want to cut across 79th?" she asked.

"You lead and I'll follow," Torrian answered.

"Dangerous words." Paige laughed. She rounded the southwestern edge of the lake and headed straight for the pedestrian crossway for 79th Street.

Just before she came up to the street, her foot connected with a tree limb hidden in the grass. She went down hard.

"Ow," Paige howled, grabbing her ankle.

Torrian dropped to his knees next to her. "What happened?"

Paige grimaced as the sting shot up from her ankle to the rest of her leg. "It's my ankle," she said. Embarrassment warmed her face.

"Let me take a look."

They were sitting out in the open, right in the middle of Central Park. They could just as well be on the JumboTron in Times Square.

"Can we go some place a bit more discreet?" Paige asked.

"You think you can walk?" he asked.

She nodded. This is what she got for being cocky.

Torrian held her gently by her upper arm and helped her

stand. Paige tested her ankle, pulling in a sharp breath at the shock of pain that zinged through her joint.

"You're going to need an X-ray," Torrian concluded.

"No way." She shook her head. One sure way to bring the discretion factor to a screeching halt was to show up at the emergency room with Torrian at her side, or worse, carrying her in his arms. "I just tweaked it a little," Paige reasoned.

"You sound like the guys on the team who don't want to admit when they're injured."

"Seriously, I'm good. I just need to sit for a minute. Help me to that shaded area over there."

It took a solid three minutes to walk the twelve yards to the oak tree. Torrian guided her to the ground and squatted. He untied her tennis shoe and removed it from her foot. The sharp pain had already faded to a dull ache, telling Paige she really had just tweaked it instead of spraining it, thank goodness.

Torrian sat her ankle on his thigh and pressed it softly with his fingers. "Tell me if I'm hurting you."

Paige studied his profile. Even with half his face hidden by the sunglasses and baseball cap, the man was still the definition of gorgeous. He didn't have to rely on his athletic ability; he could still make millions as a model.

He slowly rotated her ankle. "This still feel okay?"

"Uh-huh," Paige murmured.

"I don't think it's broken or sprained," he said, but he didn't let go of her leg. Instead, his hand moved farther up, caressing her calf muscle. It inched higher as he moved in closer, stretching his torso over hers. Paige leaned back, her nipples instantly tightening at her back's first contact with the cool, dewy grass. Or maybe it was the anticipation of feeling Torrian's solid chest against her.

He stopped mere inches from her face, his hand traveling

up to her thigh. "Tell me the truth." He grinned. "You had this in mind when you asked me to join you on your morning run, didn't you?"

"Busted," Paige said with a breathy laugh before reaching up and capturing his lips in a slow, delicious kiss. Torrian cradled her head in his palm and followed her the rest of the way down to the ground. His tongue danced in a hypnotic rhythm with hers, moving in and out and around and around in slow circles. He tasted like peppermint mixed with coffee, a heady combination that had Paige emitting low moans that traveled from the base of her stomach and up her throat.

His hand moved from her thigh to her stomach, trailing just along the edge of her shirt's hem. He smoothed his warm palm over her skin, moving to the side of her waist and squeezing.

"You're so soft," he whispered into her mouth.

Paige couldn't speak. She wanted to feel. Just feel.

His hand inched farther up, stopping just below her breasts. Paige's back arched in anticipation; her body eager to feel the caress of his large hand on her breast. But it moved in the opposite direction, going back to her side.

Paige groaned.

"We don't want to go there in the middle of the park," Torrian said.

He was right. Damn him for it, but at least he was thinking. Torrian released her mouth and stretched alongside her. Paige's entire body throbbed in the afterglow of his kiss.

"Who knew exercising could be so much fun," Paige said with a breezy sigh.

"Beats the hell out of a Sabers practice," he replied.

"Thanks." Paige laughed. "Nice to know I'm more appealing than a bunch of sweaty, dirty football players."

"A million times more appealing," Torrian said, placing a quick peck at her temple.

"It must be driving you crazy to be away, though, isn't it?"

"Any player would rather be on the field than sitting on the IR list, but being here with you is a nice alternative."

He dipped his head and caught her lips in another sweet, unhurried kiss. Despite the leisurely pace, he still caused adrenaline to pulse throughout Paige's bloodstream. When he finally came up for air, Torrian was breathing as hard as she was.

"I don't see that getting old anytime soon," he said.

"Neither do I," Paige agreed.

If anyone had told her just one week ago that she would be lazing in the grass with Torrian Smallwood, his lips seeking hers every two minutes, Paige would have hurt herself laughing. The surrealness of the moment couldn't take away from one undeniable reality: neither of them could get enough of each other.

Torrian pushed himself up on one elbow and stared down at her. She could just make out his hazel eyes behind the sunshades he still wore. "You sure your ankle isn't hurting?" he asked, concern soaking through his voice.

"It's throbbing just a little, but it'll be okay," Paige assured him. "Believe me, I've done much worse to it."

"Just let me know if it needs another kiss to make it better."

"Any more of your kisses, and we'll never get up from here," Paige said.

"You say that as if it's a bad thing." He grinned.

Paige put a hand to his muscled chest. They really had to get moving before they spent the rest of the day stealing kisses under this shady oak tree. "Didn't you say you had an appointment later this morning?" she asked.

"Yeah. The team doctors want to check my injury." He pushed himself up from the grass, and capturing her outstretched hand, gently pulled her from the ground.

As she dusted off the back of her running shorts, Paige gingerly applied pressure to her ankle, sighing in relief when nothing more than the diminishing dull ache remained.

"Is it okay?" Torrian asked.

She nodded. "You up for some breakfast?"

"I probably should head to the Sabers facility." He took her hands and brought them up to his lips. "Can I convince you to have dinner with me tonight? I want to give you a sneak peek at the Fire Starter Grille."

"Oh, a sneak peek. I'd be honored."

"Good," Torrian said with a final quick kiss. "I'll see you tonight."

Chapter 13

"This place is amazing," Paige said, her eyes still roaming around the dimmed main dining area of the Fire Starter Grille.

"Thank you," Torrian answered, following her gaze. With only three more weeks until the grand opening, the renovations were nearly complete.

"You must be nervous," Paige said.

"Not nervous, just excited for Deirdre. She's wanted this for a long time. Wine?" he asked, holding out the bottle he'd selected from the restaurant's extensive selection.

"Thank you," Paige said, retrieving her glass and bringing it in for a sip. Her eyes closed and she let out a soft mewl. "Delicious."

For a moment, all he could do was stare at the look of absolute bliss on her face. His mind immediately conjured other things he wanted to do that would elicit that same expression. His gut clenched at the prospect.

Torrian had to clear his throat before speaking. "That one is from the northern region of Italy. The wine cellar is one of the most diversely stocked in the city."

"Which is saying a lot, because New York restaurants have some of the best wines in the country."

"It was expensive bringing in selections from so many different regions of the world, but the consultant assured me the wine list was the way to get the clientele we're seeking into the restaurant."

Paige nodded. "I've reviewed a lot of places, and the wine pairings make a huge difference. It was a good investment."

Deirdre came out of the kitchen, and set the tray she carried on a nearby table.

"Here we go." She removed the single rose vase in the center of their table and replaced it with a triangle-shaped plate that held a baked artichoke drizzled with an orange-colored sauce. She sat a smaller bowl of drawn butter next to it. "Sorry I have to serve the first and second courses simultaneously, but I'm late for my study group."

"Don't be silly," Paige said. "I feel like a queen already."

"That's perfect, since I happen to think this meal is fit for royalty," Deirdre returned with a grin. Before each of them, she placed plates of perfectly grilled filet mignon, seasoned asparagus spears and potatoes so thinly sliced that the plate's etched Fire Starter Grille logo showed through.

"Bon appétit," she finished. She turned to Torrian. "Once you're done with the appetizer and main course, I have dessert in the cooler." She turned back to Paige. "Enjoy your meal."

"I know I will," Paige answered. "Thank you so much for preparing this, Deirdre."

"Thank you for coming." She gave them another half bow and turned to leave, but not before giving Torrian a sly wink.

"Your sister is so sweet," Paige said.

"Dee's good." Torrian nodded in agreement. "She also happens to be an awesome chef."

Torrian rose from his chair and dragged it around the table until he was about a foot from her. As he sat, he reached over and pulled a leaf of artichoke from the cluster. He dipped it into the drawn butter, and cupping a hand under the other, held the vegetable out to her.

With a gleam in her eye, Paige leaned forward and captured the leaf between her lips. Slowly, she dragged her teeth along the leaf, pulling the vegetable's tender flesh into her mouth.

The sight was so damn erotic that Torrian became instantly hard.

"Mmm," she moaned, closing her eyes. Torrian nearly matched her sound, savoring the look of absolute ecstasy on her face. "That's good," she groaned.

She reached over, grabbed a portion of the artichoke and dipped it. Then, mimicking his movements, held it out for him to sample. Torrian's teeth sank into the warm, supple flesh and he dragged it from the leaf. The artichoke melted in his mouth.

"Good, isn't it?"

"Unbelievable," he answered.

She tried to pull her hand away, but Torrian captured it. A drop of butter glistened on the tip of her knuckle. He brought her hand to his mouth and lapped up the butter with his tongue, relishing the salty taste combined with Paige's unique flavor.

"That was even better," he said, the words barely making it past the lump of desire lodged in his throat.

His eyes locked on hers, seeking permission. She answered with a subtle nod and leaned in close.

Torrian captured her lips, immediately pulling the bottom one into his mouth and sucking. The saltiness of the butter, mixed with her intoxicating essence, was hypnotic. He thrust his tongue in and out of her mouth, swirling it around, pulling at her tongue, relishing the taste.

Paige mewled softly. It sent his blood spiking.

He leaned until their chests touched. Her nipples were hard pebbles under her thin, silky blouse. They branded his chest, eliciting the most erotic thoughts imaginable. In his mind he saw himself draping her across the table, hitching up that sexy black skirt she was wearing and spreading her legs wide. His erection strained to the point of pain.

"Torrian," Paige gasped, pulling away. She panted, her chest rising and falling with each breath. "If we don't stop, our steaks are going to be too cold to eat," Paige said through a hoarse whisper.

"I couldn't care less about the steak."

"Speak for yourself," she said with a breathless laugh. She put her hand on his chest and gently pushed him back.

Torrian obeyed, even though he wanted nothing more than to shove the food to the floor and clear a place for her seduction. He topped off their wineglasses and they dived into their meal. The steak had cooled slightly, but he was still so overheated by their kiss that Torrian hardly noticed it.

"This is an excellent cut of beef," Paige commented. "You are serving some top-quality food here."

"We have to. Deirdre's good, but she isn't a big-name chef yet. My name is going to get them in the door, but we've got to have great food in order to keep them coming back."

"You have absolutely nothing to worry about, Torrian. The food is outstanding, the wine list is fabulous and the ambience is superb. I think you'll be pleased with my review."

"You know you don't have to be anything but honest."

"I don't know any other way to be," Paige answered. "It will not be hard to write an honest, excellent review."

They reached for their glasses at the same time and each sipped their wine, sharing matching smiles over the rim of their stemware. Apprehension tightened his chest as he geared up for what he was about to do. He knew he had a fifty-fifty chance of getting a flat-out rejection, but he'd never been one to let a bit of humiliation stop him.

"Paige?"

"Yes?" She lowered her glass and brought another bite of steak to her lips.

Torrian placed his elbows on the table and folded his hands. "I was hoping you would join me at my house in the Hamptons this weekend," he said.

Her chewing slowed; Torrian could see her swallow. She picked up her glass and took another drink. His heartbeat thudded in his ears as he awaited her answer.

"Uh, wow," she said, setting the glass on the table.

"If this is moving too fast for you, just tell me." He caught her hand and brought it to her lips. "But I want to spend time with you. *Real* time with you."

"The kind of time where we get naked together?" she asked with a bluntness he'd witnessed on her blog, but not as much in person.

Torrian had to pull in a breath; an attempt to calm himself at the image her statement summoned in his brain.

"Only if that's what you want," he forced himself to answer in the most nonchalant tone he could muster. Every part of his being was screaming to spend the entire weekend with her naked in his arms. "I don't want to pressure you into doing anything you don't want to do, but I think you would enjoy my house at the beach, with or without clothing," he tacked on with a smile. It got him the reaction he'd wanted: a return smile.

"I would have to think it over," she said.

"Well, if it's any incentive, I received an invitation from Stephen Cambridge for a party he's having at his place. I did tell you we're neighbors, right?"

Her eyes widened like beautiful saucers. "This is black-mail."

"Kind of," he admitted. "I was thinking this would be a great way for you to get some face time with him. Remind him of how fabulous it would be if he picked up your column for syndication."

Paige lowered her fork without eating the sliver of potato she'd stabbed. "You do not play fair," she said.

"Not when it's about getting what I want," Torrian told her.

"Do you think you can get an invitation to the party?"

"The invitation is already there. Cambridge was excited I finally accepted. Whenever he's invited me to one of his parties, I've had to decline. I'm hardly at my place in the Hamptons." He settled his elbows on the table. "So, what do you say? You can come as my date," he said, getting a slight thrill just at the thought of walking into a party with Paige at his side. The instant sag of her shoulders dimmed his excitement just a bit.

"Discretion, remember?" she reminded him.

They were back to that. Torrian stifled a sigh. "We don't have to go as an official couple," Torrian said. "We can just tell people that it's more promo for the show. This can be just another one of those public appearances where you have to tolerate my presence," he teased. "What do you say, Paige?"

She returned his grin, her eyes bright with laughter. "I guess I can suffer through it, for the sake of the show, of course."

"So, is this a yes?" he asked.

She stared at him from her seat across the table, and Torrian wanted nothing more than to lean over and capture her lips in another kiss.

"Yes," she said.

A mixture of relief and excitement bubbled up in his blood.

He went for his fork again, his appetite for his steak returning now that he'd gotten that out of the way.

"Torrian?"

The softness of her tone brought his head up. "Yeah?"

"My answer would have been yes even if we were not going to the party."

Torrian placed his fork on the white linen without touching his food.

"I don't want you to think the opportunity to meet Stephen Cambridge is the only reason I accepted your invitation. I said yes because I want to be with you."

Torrian pushed the plate aside, leaned over and gave her the kind of kiss that would last them both until they were finally in each other's arms.

Paige arrived at the studio less than a half hour before they were scheduled to go on the air. She ran to makeup where they quickly transformed her from tired with puffy eyes to runway beautiful. She so needed to bring the makeup crew home with her.

The hairstylist did a final flip with the curling iron, and hit the back of the chair. "You're ready."

"Thanks, Cynthia," Paige said, hopping out of the chair. She reached the kitchen with only seconds to spare.

"Don't ask," she told Torrian. Paige tied the apron around her back and pasted on a smile.

"Rolling," the segment producer said, followed immediately by the anchor woman who started, "This is the third of our five-part competition between Sabers wide receiver Torrian Smallwood and popular entertainment writer Paige Turner. Last week, our judges had a hard time deciding between Torrian's homemade cream of mushroom soup and Paige's chicken and sausage gumbo, but the gumbo won out, tying the score at one apiece and winning $20,000 for each charity, courtesy of Meyer cookware.

"Today is the all-important entrée, and if the aroma is any indication, this will be another hard-fought battle. What are you cooking for us today, Torrian?"

The camera zeroed in on his face, giving Paige a chance to throw the first of her ingredients for her artichoke-stuffed chicken into the skillet. "I've got one of the signature dishes that will be served at the Fire Starter Grille, veal cutlets with a merlot sauce.

"I seared the cutlets on each side, and now I'm going to add the ingredients for my sauce." He tossed minced garlic into a pan of sizzling oil, the hiss being picked up by the overhead microphone.

"And what about you, Paige?" came the anchor's voice.

"I've got chicken breasts stuffed with artichoke hearts," Paige answered. "This is one of my favorite recipes. The key is to pick chicken breasts that are close in size so they'll all cook evenly."

"Good tip, Ms. Turner." Torrian grinned from behind his cooking station.

"Happy to share, even with the competition," Paige answered.

"We'll check back with you two in the second half-hour." Laughter could be heard in the anchor woman's voice.

"We're out," the segment producer said.

Paige expelled a huge sigh and slouched her shoulders. Torrian was at her cooking station in seconds.

"What happened to you this morning?" he asked.

"What *didn't* happen?" Paige said. She shook her head, thinking about the call from her mother. Her dad had to be switched to yet another medication for his hypertension, after the latest one started showing side effects. "It was just one of those mornings when everything that could go wrong did."

"Is there anything I can do?" he asked.

"Burn your veal cutlets."

"Nice try." Torrian laughed. "Seriously, if there's anything I can do, just let me know."

Paige shook her head. "I'm heading back home once we're done here. I've got to finish up my next column, and then," she lowered her voice, "I need to pack for a little weekend trip I'm taking to the Hamptons."

"Hmm…sounds interesting," Torrian said.

"I have a feeling it will be. You're picking me up at the corner of 17th and 3rd, right?"

"If you say so." He shook his head. "It kills me that I can't pick you up in front of your building."

"Torrian—" Paige started.

"But I know we have to be discreet," he said. "The Torrian Smallwood supporters would be so disappointed if they found out about us. Have you checked your blog lately? People have taken sides and they are not letting up."

"I have my own share of supporters, thank you very much," Paige said, turning back to her cooking station.

"Oh, I know. And they all think you're going to kick my butt."

"Told you my readers were smart." Paige winked.

They finished up their entrées and arranged three plates for this week's judges. One was the executive chef of one of New York's trendiest restaurants, another was a local councilman, and the third was Thelonious Stokes, from the Sabers. Paige had balked at having one of Torrian's teammates as a judge, but Theo Stokes had assured her that it was to her advantage. He was always hard on Torrian, which was probably why Torrian had complained just as much as Paige had.

"And we're back with the judging portion of this week's food challenge." The three judges were introduced. Paige had to admit that Theo Stokes was nearly as gorgeous as

Torrian, even though his bulging muscles made him look twice Torrian's size.

"Let's start with dish A, the veal cutlets with merlot sauce."

As the judges sampled Torrian's dish, Paige looked over at him and found him staring back at her with his arms crossed over his apron-covered chest and a wry grin on his lips. He winked at her.

"This has to be Ms. Turner's dish," Theo called from the judge's table. "You can't convince me that Torrian cooked this." A flurry of chuckles sounded around the studio.

The judges sampled her dish next, and Paige couldn't help but feel a twinge of anxiety. Despite the change in her relationship with Torrian, this was still a competition, and with the news about her dad this morning, Paige was even more determined to raise money for the Artist Medical Fund. As a retired jazz musician, her dad had no health insurance until he turned 65 and could apply for Medicare. Paige knew having to play around with various combinations of medicines to control his high blood pressure was draining her parents' finances, even though neither would admit it.

The judges finished their sampling and jotted their decisions on the score sheets.

"We will have the results of this round after the commercial break," the anchor announced.

"We're out. Back in three," the producer said.

Theo left the judging table and headed straight for them. "What's up, Wood?" he greeted Torrian, slapping hands and pulling him in for a half hug. He quickly turned to Paige and held out his hand to her. "Good morning. I'm Theo."

"No introduction needed," Paige answered, accepting his hand. "Especially to a Sabers fanatic."

"I've become a Paige Turner fanatic," he said. "I'm hooked on your blog."

"No fair," Torrian called. "We've got some favoritism going on here."

"Stop whining," Theo said. "Believe it or not, I had a hard time choosing. You sure your sister didn't come in and make that dish earlier this morning?" he asked, eyeing Torrian suspiciously.

"Didn't know I could throw down like that in the kitchen, did you?"

Theo pointed his thumb at Torrian. "How do you put up with this nonsense?"

"It's not easy," Paige answered.

"I heard there was some drama on the flight home from the San Diego game," Torrian said, changing the subject.

"Oh, yeah, you won't believe what Cedric did this time." Torrian rolled his eyes.

"Thirty seconds," the producer called.

"I'll tell you when we're done," Theo said, and dashed back to the judges' table.

"I knew it," Paige said.

"What?"

"That guys gossip just as much as women do."

He snorted. "Women don't have a thing on men, especially when it comes to the Sabers' locker room."

"You think there's any gossip about us?" Paige asked.

But before he could answer, the anchor said, "And we're back."

Each judge discussed the merit of each dish, but in the end, Torrian's veal cutlets won out.

"Remember to tune in for the all-important dessert competition," the anchor finished, then the camera switched back to the news desk.

"Congratulations," Paige said.

"No hard feelings now that I'm up two to one?"

"I don't know about that," she said. "I really wanted to win this week."

"Maybe we can practice this weekend. I'll make sure to bring a little extra chocolate."

"That sounds…um…nice," she answered.

"It's going to be a whole lot better than just nice," Torrian answered.

Tiny shivers cascaded down Paige's spine. Just behind them, a throat cleared. Paige and Torrian jumped back and turned.

Theo stood a few feet away. "Before I go back to my place for a cold shower," Theo said. "I wanted to know if you wanted me to wait for you."

Oh, my God. Paige's heart stuttered to a stop.

"Don't worry about it," Theo said. He hooked his thumb in Torrian's direction. "He's the only one I would tell your secret to anyway."

"Give me a minute," Torrian said to his teammate.

Theo nudged his head toward a door. "Might want to find a broom closet if you don't want anyone else barging in on your little discussion."

Paige let out a deep breath. "Great," she said.

"Don't worry about Theo. He knows how to be discreet," Torrian assured her. "Go back to your apartment and pack your things. I'm picking you up at two this afternoon. We should be in the Hamptons before four."

"I'm looking forward to it," she said, but Paige refused to give in to the urge to kiss him. They had to be more careful. Although, the harder she fell for Torrian, the fuzzier her reasons for hiding became.

Chapter 14

Paige stuffed the yellow-and-green bikini in her bag and immediately snatched it out. The barely there bikini would send the wrong message. It just screamed *Rip me off*. She shouldn't be so blatant.

"Face it, you know you're going to sleep with him," she said to her reflection in her bedroom mirror.

Paige knew exactly what she was saying yes to when she'd accepted Torrian's invitation to spend the weekend. Maybe if there wasn't this surge of sexual tension radiating between them every time they were together, she could at least pretend to be clueless about what would occur at his home in the Hamptons.

"Still, you don't have to advertise it." She stuffed her more sedate brown swimsuit in with the bikini. "There," Paige said. "Leave a bit to the man's imagination."

Paige felt another slight thrill that he'd invited her to join him. Besides being one of the sexiest, most alluring men on the planet, Torrian was actually fun to be with. She'd erroneously believed he'd have a jock personality, but nothing could be farther from the truth. It was both surprising and refreshing.

Paige's cell phone rang. She went back into her bedroom to retrieve it from where she'd tossed it on the bed. Torrian's cell number illuminated the screen.

"Hello," she answered.

"Are you almost ready?"

"Almost," Paige said. "I hope you have enough room in your trunk for all my bags."

"We're going for only a couple of days," he said.

"I'm just joking," Paige laughed. "I packed extremely light."

"That sounds promising," he said after a pause, his voice an entire octave lower. "I'll pick you up in less than ten minutes."

"I'll be at the curb with my bags."

Paige gave a last check around the apartment to make sure she'd turned off everything and unplugged most of the appliances. When she exited her building and walked a half block down, a black BMW was waiting at the curb on 17th Street. The passenger-side window lowered. Paige poked her head in.

"Leave your bag on the curb, I'll get it."

"Don't be silly, Torrian. Just pop the trunk and I'll throw my bag in."

Paige could sense his gallant and sensible sides warring with each other. Sensible won out. He popped open the trunk. She placed her bag next to a black leather duffle. Torrian had already opened the passenger-side door from the inside. Paige slipped into the car and was greeted with a deep kiss.

"You look amazing."

"In a skirt and flip-flops?"

"In anything."

This man was way too smooth for her peace of mind. Paige knew he would have her out of her panties in record time. Pinpricks of anticipation skittered along her skin. Now that she'd decided to give in to the desire to sleep with him, she couldn't wait for it.

"How long until we get to your place?" Paige asked.

"If traffic cooperates we should be there by four. We'll have to stop at a grocery store to stock up on supplies for the weekend. I used to have a housekeeper on standby, but since I rarely use the house, it wasn't practical to keep her on."

She was curious, "Why don't you use the house more often?"

He shrugged with the arm that was expertly guiding the sleek automobile through traffic, "I'm not really a beach person."

"Which begs the question…"

"Why have a house at the beach." He laughed, then shrugged. "I succumbed to the status game. Back when I bought it, having a home in the Hamptons meant you'd reached some invisible rung on the ladder of success."

"It sounds as if that doesn't matter to you anymore."

Another shrug. "It took me a while to realize it, but I finally figured out that money isn't everything."

"It is nice to have, though," Paige felt the need to point out.

He looked over at her, his eyes crinkling at the edges. "Yes, it is nice to have, but not for the reasons I used to believe. It used to be all about showing what I could buy. If one of my teammates bought a car, I bought a bigger one. A house on the beach? I had to get one, too." He shook his head. "None of that stuff is important. As long as my sister and nephew are taken care of, it's all good."

She stared at him for a few moments, ruminating over all

she'd learned about him over the past few weeks. "I pegged you all wrong," Paige said. "You're the complete opposite of a self-centered jerk."

He laughed. "So that's what you thought of me?"

"Most definitely," she admitted. "In my book you fell into the category of pompous, professional athletes who used your God-given talent to get rich and become a jerk."

"Ouch. Just a bit harsh."

"It is. You've opened my eyes, though."

He reached over and covered the hand in her lap. "I'm happy you gave me the chance to."

The drive from Manhattan to the eastern edge of Long Island was a nice change from her usual view on the subway. As they sailed along the Long Island Expressway, Paige allowed the soothing jazz streaming through the BMW's speaker system to lull her to sleep. After what felt like only a few minutes, she heard in her ear, "Wake up, sleepy head."

Paige blinked rapidly several times. She looked out the window, her eyes zeroing in on a gorgeous wooden home with huge windows.

"We're here already?"

"Actually, it took longer than expected. We ran into a bit of traffic, but you slept through it."

Torrian exited the car and came over to her side, opening the door for her.

"I'm sorry," Paige said, accepting the hand he offered.

"No apology necessary. Your top kinda got twisted up there. I had a good view the entire drive."

"Pervert." Paige laughed, adjusting her top. "What about the groceries?"

"I figured I could go back out once we got here. You can take the time to nap."

"I feel awful for falling asleep. I just had so much work

to do after this morning's show, and I wanted to finish it so I wouldn't have to do any while we're out here."

"Good, because I don't want to share you with work."

They entered the house and Paige took a swift intake of breath. It was exactly the way a house at the beach should be decorated, with soft cool colors of blue, green and sandy brown. The wide-open space was sprinkled with several sets of seating areas instead of a formal living room. The area was made for mingling.

"This is lovely."

He stopped and looked around for a moment as if he was just really seeing the place. "I guess it is."

"You really need to take the time to enjoy some of the luxuries you've been blessed with."

His eyes traveled the length of her body. "I plan to," he said, his voice low, seductive.

A flush of heat swarmed over Paige's body. She knew the instant blush was evident on her skin. She had a feeling she'd be doing a lot of that this weekend.

"So do I," she said. She was just as excited at the prospect of enjoying his body, and was woman enough to let him know it. She'd told him early on that when they decided to make love, it would be a mutual decision. She was not going to play games.

Torrian blew out a deep breath. "Do you want to see the rest of the place?"

"Or."

His brow hitched.

"We can do this," Paige said. She brought her hand up and grabbed hold of his neck, pulling his head down to her. She heard the thud of the duffle bag he'd brought in from the car falling at their feet. Torrian's hands found their way to the small of her back, then lower, cupping her backside and pulling her in close contact with his hardening body.

Paige moaned as intense pleasure cascaded through her veins. His mouth was decadent, the feel of his body pressed up against hers: pure sin.

She explored his mouth with her tongue, tasting the chocolate he must have consumed on the drive over. It was the absolute best-tasting chocolate ever.

Torrian wrenched his mouth from hers and went for her throat, laving at her skin with his skillful tongue. "God, you taste good," he breathed. He got a firmer grip on her butt, then slid one hand down the underside of her thigh, hooking it behind her knee and pulling her leg up.

Paige gasped as her core came in direct contact with his erection, their clothes the only thing separating them from ultimate pleasure.

"I want you naked," Torrian whispered in her ear.

Paige nodded. She couldn't speak actual words to save her life.

Torrian lifted her up and she wrapped her legs around his waist. Paige could feel his muscles bulging underneath his shirt. She ran her hands along his back, her own body shivering in expectation of what his barely contained power could do to her once it was unleashed.

Torrian carried her down a hallway into a huge, airy bedroom with floor-to-ceiling windows overlooking a wide expanse of beach. He deposited her onto the bed, pulling his shirt over his head and flinging it across the room.

"Wait," Paige said. "We're not going to do this in front of all these windows, are we?" She wasn't a complete prude, but she was no exhibitionist either.

A grin formed on Torrian's lips. He walked over to the far wall and flipped a switch. Rattan window shades descended from a narrow slit in the ceiling, covering the windows and leaving a warm glow of light.

"Is that better?" he asked, working free the buckle at his waist as he strolled back to the bed.

"Much," Paige answered. She scooted up, bracing her back against the mountain of pillows.

Torrian nodded toward her. "You want to take off that top, or do you want me to do it?"

Paige didn't feel an ounce of self-consciousness as she reached for the hem of her sleeveless top and pulled it over her head. She tossed it next to where he'd deposited his shirt on the floor and settled back against the pillows.

"Your turn," she said.

His brows rose with a surprised grin. "Oh, is that what we're doing here? You want a little striptease."

"Well, when you invited me here, I expected entertainment as part of the package."

"I'm not much of an entertainer," he said. His unzipped his pants and pushed them down past his hips. His erection strained under the confines of his boxers. Paige's mouth dried up at the sight. She wanted that *so* bad and *right* now.

"Um, I think most of your fans would disagree," she said, trying to concentrate on their little game instead of his body. "You're very entertaining on the football field," she said, bringing her eyes back up to his face. The smile she found there was inspiring.

"I guess there are some similarities between this and football. I strive to do my best in both arenas."

Paige held up one finger as he knelt next to her on the bed. "One difference," she said. "This time you're guaranteed to score." She plunged into a fit of giggles at Torrian's eye roll. "I know that was so cheesy. Sorry, I couldn't help it. It was just too perfect."

"Kind of like this spot on your neck." He dived for the spot just behind her ear and nipped at her skin.

Paige angled her head to give him better access, her eyes

closing as pleasure seized her. He knew just when to go from biting to licking to sucking. He trailed his tongue from her neck to her collarbone, pulling the strap of her bra down her arm in the process.

"I can't take much more of this," he said.

Paige brought her hands to his chest and gently pushed him away. She knelt in the center of the bed and brought her hands behind her back, releasing the single clasp and letting the bra fall from her breasts.

Torrian's chest expanded with his huge, audible intake of breath. He came up on his knees; he was so close Paige could feel the heat from his body. She took his hands and brought them to her breasts, shutting her eyes and letting her head fall back as she pressed her hands over his. He played upon her skin, squeezing, releasing, applying more and more pressure with every clasp of his huge palms.

He went for her throat again, nuzzling the spot that had come to expect his touch. The erotic swipes of his tongue along her skin, the roughness of his fingers as they pinched her nipples, the pressure of the erection that stirred back and forth against her stomach, wrangled a moan from deep within her throat.

Torrian's hands moved from her breasts to her waist, then around to the small of her back where he undid the clasp of her skirt. He unzipped and pushed the garment down, dragging her silk panties with it. He leaned her back upon the pillows and pulled her clothes the rest of the way.

Paige lay before him completely naked, her skin burning with the need to have his hands all over her.

For long, passion-filled moments, Torrian just stared at her, his heated gaze scorching. "God, you're beautiful," he breathed.

Paige closed her eyes and inhaled deeply, her chest expanding. Her body tensed as she felt his fingers graze lightly along her throat. They traveled down the center of her body, through the valley between her breasts and over her stomach, which tightened under his touch. His fingers lingered, smoothing up and down her ribs, then went lower, closing over the spot between her legs. His palm pressed against her, one finger slipping between her folds to circle her clitoris.

Her body arched to meet his erotic caress, a soft cry escaping her throat. Torrian pinched the silken bundle of nerves between his thumb and forefinger, then slipped a single finger inside, coaxing another cry from her. All of her muscles spasmed simultaneously. Paige could hardly breathe, her senses concentrated on that one spot.

The tip of his tongue found her breasts, swirling around one nipple and then the other, sucking the distended tip into his mouth and tugging with just enough pressure to wrench another moan from her. His fingers continued to play between her legs, slipping in and out with increasing speed.

Pleasure, exquisite and intense, began to build low in her belly. Every muscle in her body tensed as Torrian's expert fingers worked their magic inside of her. Her body clenched and Paige exploded, sharp white streaks of light shooting behind her closed eyelids.

She fell back onto the bed with a satisfied groan, her body like putty.

"Oh, my God," she breathed.

Torrian lay beside her, strumming his fingers up her body to caress her breasts. "You do know that was only the beginning, right?" he whispered against her jaw.

Another ripple of sensation flowed over her body at his softly spoken promise.

He rolled off the bed and went for the pants he'd tossed on the floor, retrieving his wallet from the back pocket. He flipped it open and pulled out a condom. He shucked off his boxers and covered himself with the latex before he reached the bed.

Paige welcomed him back with a deep, soul-melting kiss. The weight of his body pushing down on her felt amazing. Torrian wrapped his arms around her and rolled over, placing her on top. His erection nudged her open, and with one swift, elegant movement, he entered her body.

Her back arched. Paige couldn't contain the shriek of pleasure that escaped as Torrian captured her waist with his hands and guided her up and down the length of him. Her body blossomed, opening for him, sucking his powerful erection deeper and deeper inside.

Twin shouts of unadulterated pleasure echoed around the room as they both yelled with satisfaction. Paige leaned forward, gripping the covers on either side of Torrian's head in her fists. His head came up and he pulled her nipple between his lips as he continued to pump into her body.

Paige pitched her head back, her neck muscles straining, the pleasure coursing through her almost too powerful to contemplate.

Almost.

With his hands on her hips, Torrian increased her pace, moving her up and down with swift, firm strokes that caused the tension pitted low in her belly to boil over and erupt in a shout of pure pleasure.

Paige collapsed on top of him, satisfaction flowing over her in waves. Finally, she rolled off him and flopped to the side, not bothering to cover herself. A relaxing contentment pulsed through her bloodstream.

A gurgle of laughter started deep in her throat. She tried to suppress it, but couldn't help it. She was overcome by a fit of silly, contented giggles.

"And you're laughing why?" Torrian asked.

"Because it's been a long time since I've felt this good," she managed to get out.

He rolled over and braced himself on one arm, looking down at her. The wide grin on his face was an outward manifestation of what she was feeling inside.

"I can live with that answer," he said. He dipped his head and covered her mouth with his.

Paige sighed into his kiss, opening her mouth and accepting his tongue. "Mmm…you do that well."

"You're pretty good yourself, Ms. Turner."

"Did you know we were going to fall into bed as soon as we got here?" she asked.

"No, I didn't know for certain," he said, nipping along her jaw. He hovered just above her, gazing into her eyes. "But it is evidence that God does indeed answer prayers, because I've been praying for this since the minute I asked you to come out here with me."

"Did I live up to your expectations?" Paige asked.

"You're so far beyond that I can't even describe it."

Paige wrapped her arms around his neck and pulled him on top of her.

"Let's see if I can help you find the words."

Paige tried to raise her eyelids, but they were not cooperating. She was completely spent, her body replete with pleasure. She heard the shower in the connected bathroom, thought about joining Torrian inside, then realized she couldn't lift herself from the bed if she tried.

She had no idea how many times they'd made love. It seemed as if they'd wasted away the entire afternoon in bed. Paige managed to open one eye and stared at the ceiling in awe. She'd just spent hours having sex with Torrian Smallwood. She tended to forget just who he was when they were together. He made it easy to forget; he didn't act like a superstar. He was just Torrian.

She looked around the room and, for just a second, allowed herself to imagine what it would be like if things became more serious between them. They had yet to talk about where things would go once they were done with the cook-off. She was hesitant to bring up the subject; afraid it would force them to make a decision neither of them were ready to make just yet.

For now, she was content to enjoy what they had found together: good conversation, great sex—okay, unbelievably amazing sex—and the ability to just have fun.

But a part of her wanted more.

Paige threw one arm over her eyes and groaned.

Don't go there, she pleaded with her brain. She would not set herself up for disappointment by expecting more than Torrian had agreed to give. She was too smart to fall into that way of thinking.

The shower stopped, and moments later Torrian walked out of the bathroom, a plush towel wrapped low across his hips.

"You're awake," he said, coming over to the bed and placing a kiss on her lips.

"You sound surprised."

"And relieved." He nodded. "For a minute there, I thought I'd killed you. You came and just passed out."

"Think about the headlines *that* story would have made." Paige laughed.

"I try to keep my private life out of the headlines," he said, nuzzling her nose. "I was going to run to the grocery store. You need anything in particular?"

"Other than another hour or so of sleep?"

He chuckled, dropping the towel and pulling on a pair of running shorts and a T-shirt. The thought of him buying groceries commando put a smile on her face.

He snatched his wallet from the dresser, came back to the bed and captured her lips in a swift but thorough kiss, whispered "goodbye," and left.

Paige waited until she heard the front door close before rolling over and burying her face in the pillow. How had she allowed herself to fall so hard so fast?

Chapter 15

Torrian switched the second canvas sack to his left hand and fished the keys from his pocket. He stopped to take a deep breath before unlocking the front door. He'd spent the last forty minutes trying to calm his body so he wouldn't rush straight to Paige when he returned. He wanted to spend the entire weekend wrapped up in those sheets with her.

A wave of need rushed over him and Torrian had to pull in another deep breath. He'd had his fair share of women. Not nearly as many as the tabloids would have people believe, but enough to be able to compare.

With Paige, there was no comparison. After less than a half hour in bed with her, every other woman he'd ever been with had been eradicated from his mind. After the fourth time they'd made love, Torrian knew she'd ruined him for anyone else for the rest of his life.

He entered the kitchen and nearly dropped the grocery bags. A firm, round butt peeked out of the open refrigerator.

Paige was wrapped in a bath towel, her feet bare. The sight was so delicious that all he could think to do was strip the towel away and turn her body inside out.

Reining in the desire that was threatening to overcome him, Torrian called out, "See anything good in there?"

She jumped and turned, a huge grin spreading across her face. "Bottled water and a box of baking soda." She laughed.

God, he loved her laugh. Especially her after-sex laugh. She seemed unable to stop herself from erupting into a fit of giggles after each climax. Desire culled in his stomach. He'd give anything to get her back in bed right now.

The low rumble of his stomach reminded him that they would both need sustenance before going for another marathon lovemaking session.

"I was thinking we could have dinner on the beach," he suggested. "There's a grill out there."

"That sounds lovely. Let me go and slip something on."

"You don't have to," Torrian quickly told her. "The beach is semi-private and the sun will be setting soon," he added, hoping to convince her to remain in her near-naked state.

She barked out a laugh. "I am not going out there in nothing but a towel." She walked toward him, stopping a scant foot away. "But I promise whatever I wear will give you easy access to whatever it is you want."

Torrian groaned. If lust could kill he would be *so* dead right now.

While Paige dressed, he got started on dinner, firing up the gas grill on the patio and throwing on the ready-made kebobs he'd picked up at the grocery store. She exited the sliding glass door wearing an airy sundress that stopped mid-thigh.

Easy access, indeed.

Her feet were still bare, and Torrian was more than just a

little encouraged at how comfortable she'd made herself in his home.

"That smells good already," she said.

"I can't take any credit this time," he answered. "They came this way."

"Well, I'd rather you spend your time with me instead of cooking."

"You're just saying that because you don't want me brushing up on my skills before the final cook-off segment," he said.

"You found me out." She laughed, leaning over to give him a kiss.

Torrian placed the kebobs on an oval platter and carried it, along with a bottle of wine, to a blanket he'd arranged on the beach. Paige followed with two wineglasses and an assortment of fresh fruit and cheese.

They settled onto the blanket and enjoyed their meal, engaging in light conversation as they feasted on the grilled meat. Paige regaled him with stories of how her brothers tortured her and her younger sister, who both now suffered from a fear of frogs and butterflies due to their antics. It was evident by the joy in her voice as she spoke of them that she cherished her family just as much as he cherished Deirdre and Dante.

She asked him to elaborate on some of the childhood stories she'd read in his book. Every time her head fell back with that unrestrained laughter, Torrian had to fight back the urge to grab her and pull her to him. He was drunk with his lust for her. Her mouth was the sweetest addiction, calling to him with a promise of more pleasure than he could handle.

"It sounds like you were quite a handful," Paige said.

"That's putting it mildly." Torrian chuckled. He pushed the plates and the platter to the side and refilled their wineglasses. Then he scooted over until he was directly across from her on the blanket. He was tired of having to turn completely because he couldn't see her out of the periphery of his eyes.

Torrian stretched out his legs next to hers and brought her feet onto his lap so he could massage the soles. A satisfied—if a bit tipsy—grin drew across her kissable lips. If he were closer to them, he would have gone in for another kiss.

"It must be something with boys," Paige said. "Though my brothers were not as bad as you were. Now I see why you're so determined to make the restaurant a success for your sister. It's too bad football keeps you too busy to join her in the kitchen. I have to admit you've got skills."

"Now that you mention it, maybe that isn't such a bad idea."

"You've still got a while before you'll have that chance, though." She took another sip.

"I wish," Torrian murmured under his breath. After a beat he said, "I have only about a year of playing ball left."

Paige tipped her head to the side, her eyes squinting in confusion. "What are you talking about?"

Torrian sucked in a huge breath and swallowed the unease that was starting to clog in his throat. He'd never said the words out loud, that his football days were nearly over. He'd known the time was coming when he'd have to reveal his condition to his teammates—to the world—but Torrian didn't think he was ready.

"There's something wrong with my eyes," he said. "It's a genetic disease called retinitis pigmentosa."

"Oh, my God," Paige breathed. She scooted closer, raised a hand to his face and caressed his jaw. "How? When?"

He tried to go for nonchalant, but it was too hard. When the words came out, Torrian could hear the unease in his own voice. "I've known for a few years. It's a degenerative disorder that's slowly eating away at my peripheral vision. It's the reason I lost the game last year."

"Oh, Torrian. You didn't lose that game."

"Yes, I did," he stressed. "I didn't see him coming up on me. If I had my full vision I could have upped my speed, swept to the right, something."

Paige scooted until she could snuggle onto his lap. She wrapped her arms around him and laid her head against his chest. She couldn't possibly know what her contact did for him. Her empathy was a salve to his battered soul.

"What's the treatment for the disease?" she asked.

"There is none," he emitted with a bite in his tone he'd been trying to curb.

Her head popped up. She stared at him, her eyes seeking. "Are you saying you'll eventually go blind?"

He shrugged. "There are studies being conducted, but who knows what'll come of them. Latoya—Theo Stokes's sister, she's my doctor—she says it won't happen for a long time—decades even, but blindness is inevitable.

"*When* I lose my full sight doesn't matter, though. I'm already a liability. If the team doctors find out about my vision, I'll be out of this league in a heartbeat."

Paige caressed his cheek, her eyes filled with understanding. "Torrian, I'm so sorry."

He nodded, not trusting himself to speak. He was torn between anger and self-defeatism, even though neither emotion was acceptable. He'd stopped looking for sources to blame a long time ago.

Stuff happened. Why should it be any different for him just because he was a celebrity?

"I shouldn't complain. I've had the chance to live my dream. And because my sister was there to make sure I didn't do anything stupid like blow all my cash on jewelry and cars, I've got enough money to live comfortably for the rest of my life."

"What does Deirdre say about all this?" Paige asked.

"I haven't told her. Dee's spent enough of her life worrying about me."

"She's going to find out eventually."

"And she'll threaten to kick my behind for not telling her sooner," Torrian admitted with a half-hearted laugh. "I'll cross that bridge when I come to it. Right now my job is to make sure one of her dreams finally comes true."

Paige caressed his jaw. "You're a good baby brother."

"I try." He smiled, admitting to himself how good it felt to have her approval. When had *that* happened? Wasn't it just a few weeks ago he'd been mouthing off about how he didn't care what Paige Turner thought of him?

"It must have been so hard to go through this by yourself." She snuggled closer.

"I haven't been totally alone in it. Theo knows, and so does his sister, who, thank goodness, happens to be an ace ophthalmologist and agreed to keep it all under wraps while she treats me. Can you imagine the media frenzy if this got out? I wouldn't be the only one blaming myself for losing the championship game last year. All of the New York Sabers' football fans would be on my ass."

"It wouldn't be as bad as all that," Paige said.

"Yes, it would," Torrian reiterated. "I've been dealing with these fans for a long time. I know how they are about their football." He sighed. "I'll figure out a way to deal with the fans when the time comes. For now, I want them all to fall in love with Deirdre's cooking, so when the news about my eyes does break, they will all love the Fire Starter Grille too much to hold any animosity toward the restaurant."

"Smart thinking," Paige said.

She linked her hands around him and squeezed him tighter. They sat wrapped in each other's arms, watching the surf crest gently against the shore. The sun had begun its descent shortly after they'd finished their dinner, and was now sinking into the graying waters of Long Island Sound.

"When you wrote that review, did you ever picture yourself sitting on the beach with me just a few weeks later?"

"Not in a million years." Paige laughed. "To be honest, I never pictured you ever reading my review."

"Why wouldn't I read it?"

She shrugged. "Just thought I was small potatoes; not enough for you to be concerned about. But look at me now. I'm on television; I have people coming up to me, asking for my autograph as if I'm some type of celebrity."

"Pretty neat, huh?"

"There's a certain appeal." She laughed.

"Try not to let the celebrity go to your head," Torrian warned. There were definite downfalls to being in the limelight.

"I'm enjoying my fifteen minutes of fame," Paige answered. "But after this is all over, I'm happy to go back to being little Paige Turner, entertainment writer. Of course, it'll be nice if a few more people were able to read it, as in just about every airline passenger in the U.S."

"You'll get the syndication deal," Torrian all but promised. "We'll make sure you get plenty of face time with Cambridge tomorrow night."

"Good. I'm going to charm the pants off him."

"Hmm…I don't know about that," Torrian said. "If you plan on charming the pants off somebody, it should be me and only me."

Paige threw her head back, her laugh echoing around the quiet beach. "I'm ready to swim. You want to join me?"

"It's October. The air may be a little warmer than usual for this time of year, but that water will be cold."

"You're not going to let a little cold water stop you, are you?" Paige asked.

Normally he would, but when she looked at him with that smile, Torrian had a hard time denying her anything. "I'll have to go and get my trunks," he said.

"You know," she pushed herself up and looked from side to side, "you were right. This beach is pretty secluded." She stood, caught the hem of her dress and brought it over her head, leaving her delectable body clad in only a skimpy pair of lilac panties. She headed for the water, and Torrian let out an audible groan at the way the lace barely covered her perfectly rounded cheeks.

Paige turned back. "Are you coming?"

"Hopefully more than once tonight," Torrian said under his breath. He scooted up from the sand and tore off his clothes, leaving a trail along the beach as he followed Paige.

They lasted less than five minutes in the frigid water.

"Those…polar bear…people…are…idiots," Paige stammered through her shivering teeth.

"So, what does that make us?" Torrian asked, swathing her in his shirt. He wrapped his arms around her and rubbed his hands up and down her arms as they trudged through the sand back up to his house.

"Even…bigger idiots," Paige said.

Torrian kissed her shoulder. "I can think of several ways to warm us up."

Ten minutes later, she was still in his arms, surrounded by a bath full of sandalwood-scented bubbles.

"Mmm," Paige moaned, settling her back against his chest. "I can't believe you don't come here more often. This is your own piece of heaven on earth."

"Maybe if I had someone to join me…"

Torrian felt her stiffen and realized what he'd just said. He was about to tell her not to read too much into it, but stopped himself. They needed to address this. He sure as hell wasn't ready to give her up anytime soon. If ever.

The admission jolted him. When had he started thinking this way? He and Paige were having a good time; it's all they'd agreed to. And by the way she'd clammed up on him, it's all she wanted.

"What did you mean by that?" she asked.

It was his invitation to backpedal. He could tell her the words had come out wrong. That she'd misunderstood him.

Instead, Torrian whispered near her ear, "Just what I said." He captured her shoulders, which were even softer after being submerged in the creamy bubbles, and turned her around to face him.

"Where do you see this all heading?" he asked.

"I don't want the competition to be the end of our time together," she said, and Torrian's heart soared.

"Neither do I. I also don't want to hide anymore," he added. "I want people to know you're my woman." He felt her instantly tense and Torrian suppressed the urge to groan. What was it with her? "What's the point in hiding, Paige? I don't care that people see us as a couple."

"I do," she said. "Torrian, I—"

He gave her a squeeze when she faltered.

"*If* I get this syndication deal, I don't want people thinking it's because of you. And *I* don't want to think it's because of you either."

He shook his head. "Paige, that doesn't make any sense. No one is going to give you a big syndication deal just because you're going out with me."

"Are you kidding? You've been in this business long enough to know how it works. You said it yourself, Stephen Cambridge has been trying to get you to one of his parties for years, and now you're going because of me. If he found out I was the sole reason you finally accepted his invitation, don't you think he'd go a few extra steps to try to impress you?

"If the Cambridge Group picks up my column, I don't

want to always wonder if it's because they liked my writing or because they were trying to get into my boyfriend's good graces."

He kissed her temple and rested his cheek on the top of her head. Her hair was so soft. Everything about her was soft, delicate. Perfect.

"Fine." Torrian released on a sigh. "I'm willing to keep things quiet a bit longer, until after you get the syndication deal."

"*If* I get the deal."

"*After* you get the deal. Cambridge would be a fool not to pick you up. I've read your stuff. Even when you're dogging out an amazing cookbook by a handsome football player, you're awesome."

"I think dogging out that cookbook was the smartest thing I ever did," she answered, leaning close until her mouth was less than an inch from his. "If I hadn't, we wouldn't be where we are right now."

Torrian squeezed the hand he'd been holding since they left his house a few minutes ago. Stephen Cambridge's place was less than a third of a mile walk. Paige had insisted it was stupid to drive the short distance, so Torrian agreed to walk if he was allowed to hold her hand up until they arrived at the house.

A thrill rushed through her body whenever she thought about the fact that he wanted to make their relationship public.

I want people to know you're my woman.

When he'd said those words, her body had instantly reacted to the possessiveness in his voice. It was primal, barbaric. And she'd loved it. He wanted her, and wanted everyone to know it.

"That's the house," Torrian said, nodding toward a palace

of glass coming up about thirty yards ahead of them. "You ready for this?"

"As ready as I'll ever be," Paige answered.

He gave her hand another reassuring squeeze. "You'll be fine." He picked up the pace, and in a matter of minutes Paige found herself entering a home unlike any she'd ever seen. The ceiling seemed to extend forever, with glass windows stretching the full length of three stories. They were greeted by two attendants. One who took her light wrap, and another who offered them a drink.

"None for me," Paige answered.

"Are you sure?" Torrian asked after ordering himself a rum and coke. "It may help with the nerves."

Paige shook her head. "With my luck, the alcohol would upset my stomach and I'd throw up all over him."

Torrian grimaced through a smile. "Okay, yeah. No drinking for you until after you've cornered Cambridge. Come on, let's mingle."

Paige anticipated a few people would recognize her from *Playing with Fire*, but she was stunned—speechless, in fact—by just how many read her weekly column and followed her blog.

This was the upper crust of New York society. She didn't recognize the faces, but the last names were those you heard about when people spoke of old money. Paige was racking her brain, trying to remember where she'd heard the name of the woman who was speaking to her right now.

"We're having a gala at the museum next weekend," the woman said. "It would be wonderful if you and Torrian could make an appearance. You've become a hit with New Yorkers."

The museum. That was it. The woman's family had funded an exhibit on Asian culture at the Museum of Natural History.

"I'll talk to Torrian," Paige answered. "I'm not sure what his schedule looks like, but if we can both make it, we will."

"Wonderful," she answered before drifting to another group of guests. Paige recognized two of them as the leads for a revival that had just closed on Broadway. Both had won the Tony back in June.

"How are you holding up?" A mixture of relief and desire licked up her spine at Torrian's soft whisper. "Are you ready to meet Stephen?"

"I guess," Paige answered, tamping down the urge to throw up, despite the fact that she hadn't eaten a thing in hours. Maybe that's why she was feeling so lightheaded.

"Just be yourself," Torrian encouraged.

She nodded as she followed alongside Torrian to the man she'd been surreptitiously studying since the moment she'd caught sight of him. He was much younger than she'd assumed, with only a slight bit of gray edging the hair at his temples.

"Torrian," Stephen Cambridge said with the enthusiasm of a true fan. "Happy you could finally make it."

"So am I, Stephen. I rarely get out here these days."

"You don't know what you're missing. I take the 'copter out here every weekend. The city is crazy."

"Well, if I had this to come to," Torrian gestured to their opulent surroundings, "maybe I would hit the Hamptons more often. Stephen, I want you to meet the other half of the *Playing with Fire* cook-off, Paige Turner."

"Yes, yes." He transferred his drink to his other hand and held out a deeply tanned palm.

As Paige shook his hand, all she could think was this man held the key to her future. After years of working like a maniac, freelancing with small, unknown publications, submitting articles to national magazines—which were summarily rejected—Stephen Cambridge had the power to make all her dreams come true.

Torrian excused himself as another guest called him away.

"I've been reading up on your work, Ms. Turner," Stephen said.

"Please call me Paige," she told him, her heart suddenly beating an aboriginal tribal dance in her chest.

Calm down.

"You have the type of writing voice that appeals to a broad audience."

"I try to keep it current but at a level that those not of the X-generation will understand."

"I hear you're the one who initially started the blogs at *Big Apple Weekly*. Pretty progressive."

"It took some campaigning, but once I convinced Jory and Peter that it would bring a younger audience to the magazine, they were on board."

"You're willing to do what you need to do in order to get the job done. I've noticed that about you. It's the same with the cook-off. You go the extra mile."

Paige clenched her fists tight in an attempt to release the built-up energy shooting through her veins. Stephen Cambridge was throwing off nothing but good vibes.

"I love what I do," Paige offered. "And I take my work seriously."

"I—"

"Stephen, can you—" A woman came up to them, interrupting his next statement. "I'm sorry," she said.

"Paige, this is my wife, Caroline."

Paige extended a hand. She had to force her eyes not to widen at the bling shimmering along Caroline Cambridge's flawlessly manicured fingers.

"I'm sorry to interrupt, but I need to steal Stephen away. A couple of our guests have to leave early."

"No need to apologize," Paige said. "I've monopolized enough of Mr. Cambridge's time."

"Not at all," Stephen said. "Actually…" He switched his drink again and stuck his free hand in his pocket, retrieving a business card. "Give my assistant a call. If you have a few minutes, maybe after one of the tapings of the show you can drop in at the office. I'd like to discuss a few things with you."

Paige clutched the business card as if he'd just handed her the Holy Grail. As the couple walked away, she expelled a huge breath. Torrian was by her side in a heartbeat.

"Well, you're still breathing," he said.

"Barely." Paige laughed.

"How did it go?" he asked. "I tried to stay close, but I didn't want to make you too nervous."

"Honestly, once we started talking, the nervousness went away. He wants me to come to his office," she said, unable to keep a huge just-got-a-car-for-my-high-school-graduation-present smile from lighting up her face. It was all Paige could do not to squeal in delight.

"Hmm, I guess we'll have to figure out a way to celebrate," Torrian drawled seductively in her ear.

Ho-kay. There would certainly be a bit of squealing in delight tonight.

"What do you say we do a bit more mingling, then get out of here? You've accomplished your goal for tonight."

"And then some," Paige said. "I never expected to come out of this with an invitation to meet with him at his office. Thank you for doing this, Torrian."

"Happy I could be of service."

Paige tried to tear herself away from his hypnotic gaze, but it was no use. She knew if anyone was paying attention to them right now, their "just costars" facade would be blown to smithereens.

He leaned closer, his forehead almost touching hers. "Forget mingling. Let's get the hell out of here."

"Torrian Smallwood!"

Paige heard Torrian hiss through his perfectly straight teeth before turning that brilliant smile on the man who'd just walked up to him. Paige recognized him; a local personal injury attorney who specialized in automobile accidents and advertised that "I don't get paid until you do" on his commercials.

If the fervor in which he attacked Torrian was any indication, he was also a huge Sabers fan. It seemed to be the case with most of the guests in attendance tonight.

The irony continued to baffle Paige. These people were some of the wealthiest she'd ever encountered. The majority of them could buy Torrian Smallwood and a number of his teammates without putting a dent in their hedge funds, yet they treated him like a god.

It couldn't be his star power that drew them in. Many of them were stars in their own right. Was it his athletic ability they found so fascinating? People glommed on to him, and Torrian handled it all with a patience and grace Paige couldn't help but admire.

Maybe that's what made him such a popular player. Paige had seen her share of obnoxious jocks who thought the sun rose and set on their behinds, but that wasn't Torrian. The most obnoxious thing he'd ever done was respond negatively to her blog, and she now knew why he'd had such a strong, knee-jerk reaction. It was more about his sister's happiness than his own bruised ego.

Paige caught his eye as he stood several yards away, signing an autograph for another face she recognized but couldn't place. Torrian sent her a sly wink as he posed for a picture.

"Paige," the heavily tanned, slightly balding man motioned for her. "Why don't you get in here?"

Paige faltered. She still wasn't used to people she'd never talked to before addressing her as if they had known her for years. She'd had the occasional fan catch her on the street, but it had been nothing compared to the notoriety she now had because of the show.

She joined the picture, and found herself being passed around to several guests who wanted pictures with the two stars of *Playing with Fire*.

"It gets easier," Torrian whispered in her ear after what she hoped was their last photograph.

"I'm not sure I'll ever get used to the attention."

"You will." He shrugged. "There are perks. You can get away with a whole lot of things you'd never be able to say otherwise."

"Like you ragging that guy over his Hawaiian shirt?" She laughed.

"Exactly." Torrian grinned. "He laughed it off like it was this huge joke, when in fact that shirt was butt ugly."

"You are so bad." Paige chuckled.

He leaned over and in a deep, seductive voice, said, "But you have to admit I'm also really, *really* good."

Tremors sailed down her spine as a concoction of something warm and tingly started brewing in the pit of her stomach.

Torrian stepped back, a touch of wicked still tipping up the edge of his lips.

"How much longer until we can leave?" Paige asked in a rush of breath.

"As soon as we can make it out the door without people harassing us," he answered.

They had to dodge a few people on the way out, but Torrian was as skillful dodging the party guests as he was dodging an opposing defense on the field. They made it back to the beach house in record time, and were naked and in his bed in a matter of minutes.

Paige awoke an hour later to the aroma of something chocolaty and...spicy?

She wrapped herself in Torrian's bathrobe and padded barefoot out of his room. She found him in the kitchen, his back to her as he stood at the island stove in nothing but a towel and the thin gold chain that had a permanent place around his neck.

Two recessed lights shone down on him. The muscles of his sculpted back undulated with his movements as he stirred something on the stove.

Need pulsed low in Paige's belly as she remembered the texture of his skin as she gripped his back while he pumped into her over and over and over. It was all soft and warm draped over hard and powerful.

Paige pulled in a loud, shaking breath. It was either that or collapse in a dead faint.

Torrian turned at her intake of breath.

"You're awake," he said, standing there looking like every single fantasy she'd ever had.

Paige stepped down the two steps into his sunken kitchen, and sauntered over to the huge marble island. It was big enough to hold a six-burner stove, and a sink with a chrome, gooseneck faucet. The island dropped off to a lower tier that seated four stools.

"It was your cooking that did it," Paige confirmed, unable to stop herself from wrapping her arms around his waist and planting a gentle kiss on the spot between his shoulder blades. His back arched instinctively and he sucked in a gasp.

"We left Cambridge's place before we could eat dessert, so I thought I'd make some for you," Torrian explained.

"You mean I get more than what I just had back there?" She tipped her head toward the bedroom.

"That was just the preview." She could hear the smile in his voice. "This, my love, is the main event."

Her heart tripped up at his endearment, but Paige staved off the enticing temptation to read anything more into it. No vows of love would be made, nor was she expecting them. They were still in the having-fun, getting-to-know-each-other stage.

Except she found herself falling in love with what she'd come to know of Torrian.

Paige closed her eyes and dropped her head upon his back. She *so* was not going there. *Please, just don't go there,* she implored, hoping her mind would listen.

"You up for something sweet?" Torrian asked.

Paige lifted her head and peered around his shoulder. He swirled a smooth, deep brown chocolate in a small saucepan. A ding sounded.

"That's my soufflé," he said, dislodging from her hold and heading for the double stacked in-wall ovens.

"Soufflé?" Paige asked.

Torrian pulled out a shallow baking pan and carried it over to the island. Inside were two ramekins holding perfectly baked soufflés.

"How did you manage this?" Paige asked with a hint of concern. She still had to beat him in a cooking contest after all.

"Sister? Chef? Any of that ring a bell?" Torrian asked.

"You're going to kick my butt in the dessert segment, aren't you?" she muttered.

"Oh yeah." Torrian laughed. "It's been a fair fight up to this point, but I've got to pull out the big guns if I'm going to win."

"This ultra-competitive streak of yours cannot be healthy."

"This ultra-competitive streak is the main reason I have a job," he said, getting back to his chocolate sauce. "Look on the bright side, at least you get a sneak peek at my final dish. You've still got time to come up with something to top this."

"Yeah right," Paige snorted. She scooted onto the bar stool next to him and propped her chin in her upturned palm. "Unless I can convince Emeril to throw on a skirt and cook in my place, I think it's safe to say this competition is yours."

"Don't feel too bad, baby. To make it fair, I'll split the last portion of the prize money with you, that way both our charities walk away with fifty thousand."

"Will you share the title of winner with me?" Paige asked.

"Heck no, I'm not that generous."

Paige scrunched her face, pulling a laugh from him.

"So, what's in the pot?" She gestured to his saucepan.

"Dark chocolate with a hint of cayenne pepper."

"Interesting combination."

"According to Deirdre, the cayenne follows almost as an afterthought, adding a kick to your taste buds."

"Am I allowed to sample?" Paige murmured.

Torrian sent her a wickedly sexy grin as he scooped up a bit of the chocolate sauce. Holding a hand under the spoon, he strolled to the bar stool where she sat.

Paige's taste buds tingled in anticipation, although it wasn't so much the chocolate as it was the man carrying it.

"Watch it," Torrian cautioned her in a low, sexy voice. "From what I hear the spiciness sneaks up on you."

"Thanks for the warning," Paige returned, her reply equally seductive.

She opened her mouth, holding Torrian's gaze as he fed her the warm chocolate. It was heaven; a decadent, silken sin upon her lips and tongue. Paige closed her eyes and moaned as the smooth chocolate traveled down her throat.

When she opened her eyes, Torrian was still in that same

spot, staring at her with a heat that surpassed the flames licking the bottom of the chocolate-filled saucepan.

"How is it?" he asked.

Paige crooked her finger. "Why don't you taste for yourself?"

He leaned over and did just that, plunging his tongue into her mouth. Their mouths danced in rhythmic unison, licking and biting and sucking and devouring.

Paige mourned the loss of his taste as Torrian pulled away. He reached over and turned the fire off under the chocolate. Then he picked up the small saucepan and brought it with him.

His grin was sinful. "Turn around," he ordered.

Paige spun the bar stool around and faced him. Still holding the saucepan in one hand, Torrian reached out to her with the other and loosened the tie at her waist. The heavy robe fell open, exposing a six-inch span of breasts and abdomen.

"Lean back," Torrian said.

Unsure of his plans, she nevertheless followed his orders. She arched her back on the lower half of the marble bar, the robe falling completed away from her breasts. Torrian stepped between her spread legs; the towel still wrapped around his waist brushed her inner thighs. He ran his hand from her neck, down her chest, to her stomach.

Paige closed her eyes, anticipating his hand reaching the spot that had become addicted to his touch. But his fingers never reached her core. Instead, a trickle of hot, silky chocolate fell upon the valley between her breasts. Paige hissed at the contact, then groaned as Torrian's tongue licked a wide path along her skin.

His erection pulsed from behind the towel, hitting Paige just where she needed it. She clamped her thighs around his waist, imprisoning him.

She heard the clank of the spoon as Torrian swirled it in

the pot of chocolate. She opened her eyes to find the look on his face intense as he lifted the spoon and drizzled a swirl of chocolate upon her breast. His tongue cleaned the chocolate from her skin, twirling from the base of her breast, and going around and around, ending at the erect nipple. He sucked it into his mouth.

Paige groaned. Her body bowed, pushing her breast up even higher into Torrian's warm mouth.

He set the pot of chocolate next to her on the bar and wrapped his free arm around her waist. He lifted her from the bar stool, and kicked the stool to the side.

"Turn around," he ordered again.

Paige looked into his eyes. His stare was so determined, so full of intent; all she could do was obey.

She turned and Torrian grabbed the robe from her shoulders and dragged it down her arms. He placed his hand on the small of her back and gently pushed her face down onto the cool marble. His tongue licked a path up her spine to the spot between her shoulder blades.

The chocolate followed.

Paige arched her back, the sensation of the cold marble on her breasts and the hot sauce on her back wrenching another moan from her. Torrian ate more of the chocolate from her skin, licking and nipping his way along her back.

Paige's body tensed in eager expectation when she felt the towel fall from Torrian's waist, putting them skin to skin. He used his legs to spread her thighs apart, gripped her hips and entered her from behind.

Paige gasped, her entire body growing taut as he plunged his full length into her over and over and over again. She gripped the edges of the countertop with both hands to steady herself as Torrian pushed deeper and higher, stronger and faster, in and out, with breath-stealing power.

Her orgasm hit with remarkable speed, the intensity nearly

blinding her. Paige's stomach clenched against the hard marble. Her muscles tightened as a second orgasm spiraled throughout her body.

Torrian collapsed onto her back, his heavy breathing evidence of the tumultuous roller-coaster ride they'd just been on. For long moments there was no sound other than their shallow, frantic pants of breath renting the air.

Paige stared out the window of Torrian's bedroom, watching the hypnotic rhythm of the waves crashing upon the beach. The illumination of the moon offered just enough light to see the gentle rush of water as it rolled in, then back out. She wasn't sure how long she'd been staring, but figured it was at least two in the morning.

Torrian's softly whispered "Are you okay?" confirmed that he was awake.

"I'm fine," Paige answered. His hand settled at her waist. "You still want this to continue when we get back to the city?" she asked.

"If you think I can just walk away from you, you haven't been paying attention," he said. He captured her chin in his hand and stared down into her face. "And I'm tired of hiding. I want people to know we're together. You know you're going to get that syndication deal on your own merit. That's all that should matter."

He was right, Paige realized. But then another thought occurred to her. "What about the show? Don't you think news of us together will undermine it? I don't want anything taking the spotlight from our charities."

"We can wait until after the show," he said. "In fact, why don't we have our coming out the night of the restaurant's grand opening? I want you to be my date."

She gazed into his eyes. "I can't think of anything I want to do more."

One of his brows quirked. "I can think of one thing."

Then he proceeded to show her.

Chapter 16

Traffic was at a standstill. It had been that way for the past two hours as the paparazzi and onlookers alike descended on the Fire Starter Grille. Everyone wanted a glimpse of the star-studded guests who'd been lucky enough to score a handcrafted invitation to the opening night/book launch bash.

Torrian sat behind the wheel of his BMW two blocks away from the restaurant's entrance. He and Paige had been parked here for the past forty-five minutes. Torrian wasn't scheduled to make his big appearance for another half hour. He'd come here early for this very purpose, to see the mass of bodies clamoring around the Fire Starter Grille.

Excitement pulsed through the city like a living, breathing thing. The restaurant opening and book signing had been the talk of the town. On the heels of his big win of the *Playing with Fire* competition, it had not been hard to keep the buzz going.

"You're not upset about how the show turned out, are you?" he asked Paige.

She lolled her head to the side and rolled her eyes at him. "How many times do I have to tell you no? Your dessert was awesome. You deserved to win. I'm just happy I had the first sample," she said with a wicked smile.

Just the mention of that night in the Hamptons when he'd licked spiced chocolate from her body caused his heart rate to spike. It was physically impossible for him to do anything but lean over and connect his lips to hers. God, this woman was sweet. She tasted like everything that was good in life.

"Thanks for sticking to your bargain and splitting the last of the prize money with me," she said.

"My pleasure," Torrian answered, going in for another kiss. It's a good thing all the attention was focused on the restaurant. Even though his windows were tinted, an observant passerby would have been treated to quite a show had they stopped long enough to peer into his car.

When Torrian finally released her lips, Paige expelled a lazy, satisfied sigh. "We can do this all night, but believe it or not, there are more important things to do."

"What could be more important than making out in my car?" Torrian asked.

She grinned, grabbed his hand and placed a kiss across the ridge of his fingers. "This is your night," she said. "It's show time."

Torrian drifted from one table to the next, personalizing the cookbooks that had already been autographed and placed on the seats of each table.

"You want this made out to you?" he asked the young girl from the New York Boys and Girls Club. The publicity department at the publishing company had glommed on to his idea of inviting not only celebrities but underprivileged kids as well to the opening night celebration. Other than his teammates, Torrian could have done without many of the A-listers on tonight's guest list. They would forget about this party after the night was over and they were onto the next big celebrity powwow. For the kids at this table, this was probably the biggest thing that would ever happen to them.

Torrian personalized the other books and made promises to drop in at the after-school camp where many of the kids spent their evenings.

Every single table in the main dining room and the private one was filled. The special invitation for tonight's grand opening was the most coveted item in New York. There had been several reports of fakes being sold on eBay, but thanks to the hologram photo of licks of fire on the back of each invitation, counterfeits were easy to spot.

The fact that so many people wanted in caused a rush of excitement to pulse throughout his body. Everyone was talking about this restaurant being New York's newest sensation. It's everything he'd wanted to give Deirdre. And his sister was eating it up.

Torrian sought her out in the sea of tables. Dee had pulled out all the stops, dressed in her executive chef's uniform, complete with the traditional pleated chef's toque atop her head. Seeing the animated smile on Deirdre's face as she talked with guests and accepted their praise made every single cent he'd pumped into this place worth it.

"You look as if you're enjoying yourself."

He turned and his heart constricted in his chest as he looked at Paige.

Even better than the feeling he got when he saw the joy on Deirdre's face was the pleasure he'd experienced when he'd walked through the smoke glass doors of the Fire Starter Grille with Paige on his arm for all his guests to see. The entire restaurant had erupted into applause at the entrance of the stars of *Playing with Fire,* but when Torrian grabbed Paige and kissed her, the crowd went absolutely wild.

Apparently, he and Paige had not done a good job of hiding their true feelings for each other. Speculation about their off-camera relationship had become hotter than the stoves on the set of *Playing with Fire.* Everyone he'd talked to tonight said their chemistry on camera was undeniable.

"So?" Paige asked. "*Are* you enjoying yourself?"

"The question is, are *you* enjoying yourself?"

"Why is that the question of the night?"

"Because I want you to be happy," Torrian replied. "More than anything. What will make you happy, Paige?"

Her beautiful brown eyes looked directly into his. "I couldn't be any happier than I am at this moment," she answered. "I'm here with you, sharing one of the biggest nights of your life. I'm adoring all my fans who are just fawning over me," she said with a dramatic fluttering of her lashes.

"Oh, yes, I've witnessed the fawning. I don't know how you stand it," Torrian teased.

"And," she continued, "I just received word that my column will be syndicated."

Torrian's mouth dropped open. "Are you serious?"

"Yes," she said, her air of nonchalance replaced with an excitement that rivaled any he'd ever seen.

"Baby, congratulations. How? When?"

"Angela just called. She said the managing editorial director from the Cambridge Group called Jory over two hours ago. Can you believe he was going to wait until I got in tomorrow to tell me?"

"He's going to be upset with Angela for spilling the beans."

"As if either Angela or I care." She leaned forward and kissed his cheek. "Torrian, this feels so amazing. I've wanted it for so long."

"Feels pretty good to have your dreams come true, doesn't it?"

"You would know," she answered, placing a sweet, gentle kiss on his lips.

God, it felt good to kiss her out in the open, without having to worry about who may be coming around the corner. It was pure heaven.

Playful clapping behind him pulled Torrian from Paige's lips. He turned to find Latoya standing a couple feet away.

"I won the pool." She did a little happy dance. "We've had one running between the doctors on my floor since the second week of the *Playing with Fire* show." She turned to Paige. "I'm Latoya Stokes. It's wonderful to meet you. You were absolutely amazing on the show."

"Thank you," Paige answered. "Did you say your last name was Stokes?"

"Yes, I'm Theo's sister," she answered.

"Oh," Paige said. "Oh," she said again with more meaning, looking between Torrian and Latoya.

"Yes," Torrian confirmed. "She's my doctor."

Latoya opened her mouth to speak, but Torrian stopped her. "It's okay," he said. "Paige knows."

"Wow. Really," she said slowly, her eyes widening. "Maybe I didn't win the pool after all. I figured you two realized you were meant to be together by the end of show four, but it must have been a lot earlier than two weeks ago if you've managed to share that," Latoya said in a lowered voice. She gave Torrian a kiss on the cheek. "I'm so happy for you, honey." She stuck out her hand to Paige. "Great meeting you. Take care of him," she warned.

"I will," Paige answered. "So—" she wrapped her arms around Torrian's neck "—is she an old girlfriend I should be jealous of?"

"Not in a million years." Torrian chuckled. "Latoya doesn't

really go for the Sabers football players. Now, the cheerleaders maybe."

"Ah," Paige said with understanding. "Well, that's good, because I don't want any other woman calling you honey."

"A jealous girlfriend." Torrian smiled, nodding his head. "I like that. Any chance I can get you to fight with a woman over me?"

"Nope." Paige laughed. "And just for future reference, I do not fight like a girl. I punch."

"Figures." Torrian laughed. "Come on, let's finally have some of this food everybody's been enjoying. We're letting the press in at nine o'clock, and I want to eat without them scrutinizing the way I chew my steak."

"The press cannot be that bad." Paige laughed.

"Yes, they can," he replied.

"Hey, wait a minute. Should I remind you that I'm a part of the press?"

"Present company notwithstanding," Torrian said, wrapping an arm around her hip and leaning in for yet another kiss.

"Smart answer, Fire Starter. Smart, smart answer."

When she was younger, Paige had never had aspirations of being prom queen—that was always her sister's thing. But after tonight, Paige could certainly see the appeal of being the girl at the center of attention.

This was the Fire Starter Grille's night, but her and Torrian's relationship had taken center stage. It's all anyone wanted to talk about. Once the talk moved from what happened behind the scenes of *Playing with Fire*, it quickly turned to her column in *Big Apple Weekly*.

Not in a million years would Paige have thought that simple, four-paragraph review of Torrian's book would have led to her being on the lips of the most celebrated people in New York City. After writing for years about the city's newest *it*—newest "it" writer, newest "it" Broadway star—*she* was the "it" on everyone's list.

The thought was heady, but Paige knew it wouldn't last. She'd never been one for the spotlight. After the novelty of this wore off, she would be more than happy to go back to being the unseen face behind *Page Turners with Paige Turner*.

"Are you almost done?"

Torrian's question knocked her out of her daydream of bright lights and movie stars. She looked down at what was left of her seared tuna.

"I could eat another bite," she said. "But I shouldn't. Besides, I want to save room for dessert."

"Yes, you do," Torrian said. "It's a surprise that you will not want to miss." He looked down at his watch, then at the door. "They're going to let the press enter in another ten minutes. I was wondering if you would come to the storage room with me for a few moments."

He had to be kidding. "Now, Torrian?" Paige whispered, looking around to see if anyone had heard his request.

A decadent smile spread over his lips. "That's not what I was thinking, but I'm damn happy to know that's the first place your mind went."

She blushed as she followed him to the kitchen. It was like a well-oiled machine. Everyone moved at a lightning-fast pace, but they were all cool and calm, their movements fluid as dozens of individual ramekins of chocolate soufflé were plated.

Paige pulled in a deep breath. Her body reacted instinctively to the dark chocolate and cayenne pepper combination.

"You did this, didn't you," she accused Torrian as he led her past the line of cooks.

"It was a special request," he answered with laughter in his voice. "Of course, I didn't tell Deirdre why I was requesting this special dessert."

"Thank God," Paige said. "I'd never be able to look her in the eye."

They arrived at the huge walk-in storage room. Large containers of spices lined the shelves.

"So, what was so important that you had to take me away from my tuna?"

"I'm going to come clean to the team doctors," Torrian said. "About my eyes. I'm going to tell them."

"When?" Paige gasped.

"At tomorrow's practice," he said. "I have a checkup to clear my shoulder to play in Sunday's game, but I can't stay with the team through the playoffs knowing I'm a liability. It isn't fair to them."

"Are you sure you want to do this so soon, Torrian?"

"It's not soon enough," he countered. "I should have come clean way before this, Paige. It's past time I do the right thing."

She stepped up to him and leaned her forehead against his. She stared into his eyes. "You're so brave."

"At the risk of ruining your image of me, no, I'm not. I'm scared out of my mind."

"Don't be. You're so much more than just football. Whatever happens, you're going to land on your feet."

He raised his head and captured her chin in his fingers. He tipped her face up, lowered his mouth and kissed her slowly, thoroughly.

"I love you, Paige."

Her breath caught in her throat, followed by a rush of emotion that brought tears to her eyes. "I love you, too," Paige said. Out of everything she'd gained from *Page Turners with Paige Turner*, he was the most precious.

"Come on." Torrian grabbed her hand. "It's time to go face the press."

Chapter 17

After only five minutes of fielding questions from the press, Torrian was ready to send them out of the restaurant. He needed to remember that the press was now his friend. The more exposure the restaurant received, the better.

"Is it true the reason you opened the Fire Starter Grille was to give your sister her own restaurant?" a reporter from the *Daily Times* asked.

"This is something I've wanted to do for a long time," Torrian answered. "My sister, Deirdre, has done a lot for me. You'll all read much more about it when you read my book. So…" Torrian clapped his hands together. "Any other questions?"

"Just one," came a voice that sent a thread of disgust through Torrian's veins. He turned and noticed Barry Stein standing at the edge of the crush of reporters, his notepad in his hands.

"Yes?" Torrian asked.

"How will your eye condition affect your work here at the restaurant?" Torrian's blood chilled. His eyes zeroed in on Stein, who continued, "I assume you plan to spend your time here during the off season. Will your…what is it?" He consulted his notepad. "Retinitis pigmentosa hinder you in any way? At the restaurant, that is. Apparently, you don't feel it's affected you on the football field since you've known about the disease for years, yet you're still on the Sabers team."

The increased mumbling among the gathered press was drowned out by the blood rushing through Torrian's ears. How in the hell did Stein find out?

"Any response, Fire Starter?" Stein asked with his signature smugness.

Torrian took a labored breath, hoping like hell it would calm his rising ire. "My condition isn't up for discussion," he answered. "Tonight is about the restaurant and the book. If you don't have questions about either of those, then I'm afraid I have nothing for you, Mr. Stein."

The questions bombarded him from all angles.

"Do you have a disease?"

"Is that why you missed so many passes this season?"

"Tell us about retinitis pigmentosa."

"How long have you known you had an eye condition?"

Torrian turned away from the barrage of inquiries that were hurled from the reporters.

"Wood." Theo caught his shoulder, but Torrian brushed him off as he headed for the storage closet.

Torrian sat on the floor with his back against the wall, his head in his hands.

How had Stein found out? They had been so careful all this time. He, Theo and Latoya had made a pact, and he'd never had reason to believe they would break it. It just didn't make any sense.

The only other person…

Torrian's head popped up.

"Hell no," he said aloud. Paige would not have sold him out. Not after everything they had been through.

But she was the only other person who knew.

And as a reporter she was the only one who had everything to gain by sensationalizing his eye condition. Her career meant everything to her, and being the source for one of the biggest stories in New York sports would be a hell of a career boost.

Torrian choked on the bile clogging his throat.

The force of Paige's betrayal cut so deep that it felt as if he'd impaled himself on one of Deirdre's freshly sharpened knives. He'd trusted her with his deepest, darkest secret, and she'd used it against him. And for what? To further her career?

Why was that such a surprise? Everything she'd done since she'd known him had been to further her career. Her review of his book, agreeing to do the cook-off, coming to his home in the Hamptons because of the invitation to Cambridge's party.

Making love to him.

He'd bet that had been just another part of the plan. She'd had her eyes set on a goal from the very beginning, and selling him out was just one more way of reaching her final destination. He wasn't naive enough to think a few nights in his bed was enough to derail her well-laid career track.

An ache vibrated throughout his body at the thought of the time they'd spent in each other's arms being anything but real. Torrian clutched his eyes tight against the pain in his heart.

There was a knock on the storeroom door.

"Torrian?"

A ferocious stab of anger pierced his chest at the sound of her soft voice.

"Torrian, are you okay?" Paige asked, stepping into the storage closet and closing the door behind her.

"Get out!" Torrian growled.

"What?"

He opened his eyes and drilled her with a deadly stare. "I said get the hell out of here." Torrian pushed up from the floor. In two strides he was in her face, backing her up until she butted against the shelf.

"You must feel really good right now. You were the first reporter to know about the biggest scandal of the year."

"Torrian, what are you talking about?"

"What I don't understand is why did you let Stein break the story? Why didn't you just save it for your own article?"

"Torrian, listen to yourself. Do you really believe I told Barry Stein about your eye condition?"

"Who else would have done it, Paige? The only other people who knew were Theo and Latoya, and they've managed to keep their mouths shut for two years. I told you a few days ago, and now the whole world knows. Doesn't take a genius to figure that one out. Hell, even a dumb jock with bad eyes can do it."

She threw her hands up in exasperation. "You just said it yourself! If I wanted to out you just to further my career, I would have broken the story myself. Why would I let Barry Stein have all the glory?"

"I don't know how you reporters operate. Maybe you're going to come out tomorrow with the story of how you were just a victim in my web of lies. Is that it? That way you don't come across as the reporter who screwed around to land the big story."

She flinched as if he'd slapped her. "Oh my God, Torrian, don't do this," she pleaded. "You cannot seriously think I would betray you like this."

"Get out," he said again.

He stepped away from her, and had to turn his back completely. Even after he'd just ordered her to do it, he couldn't stomach seeing her walk away.

Torrian had hoped she would plead with him again. He wanted her to do something that told him she was the least bit sorry for what she'd done. But she didn't say anything. The only sound was the soft click of the door closing behind her.

Torrian went back to his place on the floor and resumed his position. Arms on his knees. Face in his hands. Pain in his heart.

Chapter 18

Torrian added another twenty pounds to each end of the bar and returned to the weight bench. He could have done this at his home gym, but he figured this would be one of the last times he would be allowed in the Sabers workout room. This was more about storing up memories than strengthening his muscles.

Theo entered the weight room. "What's going on with you, Wood? You've been avoiding my calls like we're two teenagers who just broke up right before the homecoming dance."

"I haven't been up to talking," Torrian bit out between clenched teeth. The bar had become harder to pump with each rep, but he wasn't about to stop now. Not until Theo got the point and left him the hell alone.

Theo grabbed the weight bar with both hands and placed it in the cradle. "Get up," he said.

With a disgusted sigh, Torrian sat up and pushed himself

from the weight bench. "I'm not doing this with you," he said, heading in the direction of the punching bag.

Theo caught his arm and whirled him around. He pointed a finger in Torrian's face. "I've covered for your ass for two years. My sister put her entire practice in jeopardy. So, yeah, you're talking."

Torrian rolled his eyes but relented. "Okay, what do you want to talk about? You already know my big secret, just like everyone else. You know what's gonna happen when I go into the exam room to meet with the team doctors. What else is there to talk about?"

"First of all, you *don't* know what the doctors are going to say."

"Oh, come off it, man. I know my career is over." Torrian grabbed the bottle of water he'd brought with him and headed for the exit.

"What about Paige?" Theo called to his back.

Torrian whipped around. "What about her?" he asked, stalking back to his teammate.

"You done with her?" Theo asked.

"What the hell do you think?" Torrian barked.

"So, that's it? You're not even going to talk this thing out with her?" Theo shook his head. "Losing your job may be out of your control at this point. But if you lose Paige, that's all on you."

"You don't lose something you freely gave up," he gritted through his teeth.

"Come on, Dawg. Do you really think she sold you out?"

"Did you do it?" Torrian asked, getting up in Theo's face.

"You really gotta ask me that?"

"You don't think Paige did it. You think it was Latoya?"

Theo's lip curled in anger. "I would kick your ass if you weren't already doing it yourself."

"What? I'm just trying to figure out who the culprit is, Theo. If you didn't do it, and Latoya didn't do it, that means the only two people left who knew anything about my eyes are me and Paige. Between the two of us, who do you think would have spilled the juicy secret to Barry Stein?" He leaned in close. "Let me give you a hint, it wasn't me."

Torrian straightened and steeled his heart against the words he was about to say. "It only leaves Paige." The thought of her going behind his back still caused a hurt Torrian doubted he'd ever be able to overcome. "Now, if you don't mind, I've got a job to lose."

He turned and walked out of the weight room for the last time as a New York Saber.

Paige rearranged the hand-sewn quilt, tucking the edges underneath her legs. She leaned against the pillows butted up against the headboard, and reached over for the tea her mother had placed on the nightstand.

Her old room felt the same, even though most of the furniture was new. The only thing that remained from Paige's childhood years was her grandmother's well-worn rocking chair.

There was a soft knock at the door. "Olivia?"

"Come in, Mom," Paige called. Her mother pushed the door open and entered the room carrying a second teacup. She went straight for the rocking chair, but Paige motioned her over.

"No, come and sit here." She patted the bed.

Marlena Turner looked good for sixty-three. She couldn't afford to torture herself with expensive plastic surgery, or even your run-of-the-mill facial. She just lived a good life, and it showed on her face.

But her eyes were sad. And Paige knew why. Marlena also

empathized with her children when they were hurting. Like today.

Her mother switched her teacup to her right hand and used her left one to run through Paige's short hair. "How is your cold?" she asked.

Paige shook her head, a self-deprecating grin on her face. "It's not a cold, Mom. We both know what it is."

"I didn't want to just bring him up," her mother replied.

"It's okay. It's been over a week. I think I can handle talking about him."

She knew she could talk about Torrian with her mother, because she'd just done the same with her sister. But unlike her mother's subtle, soothing encouragement, Nicole had demanded answers. Paige went through the entire conversation she'd just had with her sister.

"Why would he believe you would be so dishonest?" her mother asked.

Paige hunched her shoulders. She'd asked herself the same question over and over again. Had Barry Stein told Torrian that Paige had been his source? Whatever his reason, Paige had come to one simple conclusion: Torrian didn't trust her. That's what mattered.

"I don't know, Mom. I thought he knew me better than that. I thought *I* knew *him* better. The one thing I do know, this hurts so much it's killing me."

"Oh, Olivia," her mother said, leaning over and enveloping her in a hug.

"It'll be okay. Eventually." Paige sniffed. "How's Dad doing?"

"He's fine." Her mother waved her off. "He's resting."

"I feel horrible. I came here to help you look after him, and you've had to look after me as much as you've had to care for Dad."

"Your father is going to be fine. Medicine has come a long

way since your grandfather's heart attack. They had your dad out of there the next day."

"It was a blessing Dad's heart attack was only a mild one, but it was a wake-up call."

"Yes, it was. No more fried food for him, no matter how much he begs. I am grateful to have you home for a bit, though," her mother said, nuzzling her forehead against Paige's.

"I'd rather come home under better circumstances, but I'll admit it's nice to be here. It would have been awful to be holed up in my apartment these past few days."

"Well, as much as I love having you here, you'll eventually break my heart and go back to New York. You need to think about how you're going to handle that."

"I know," Paige answered. It's something she'd been mulling over since returning to New Orleans. Just because she'd packed a bag and left her problems, it didn't mean they wouldn't be waiting for her when she returned.

"I'll have dinner ready in about an hour," her mother said, kissing Paige's forehead as she rose from the bed.

"I can help," Paige offered.

"No. You've done your share of cooking over the past few weeks." Her mother laughed. "Stay here, rest."

"I love you, Mom."

"I love you, too, baby."

For long minutes after her mother's departure, Paige thought back on how many times this scenario had played out between them. From her elementary school days when she cried nightly over kids teasing her inability to read to broken hearts in high school. Her mother had always been there to soothe and comfort, and offer her special brand of support.

It would be so easy to stay here and soak in all that love and consoling, but Paige knew what she had to do. She had to return to New York. There was unfinished business to attend to, a career to grab hold of.

This time back home had given her a chance to engage in some much-needed soul searching. Torrian's accusations played back and forth in her head. Paige realized he would not have accused her of such vile things if she had not given him good cause. She thought about some of the decisions she'd made over the years. How many times had she been uncomfortable with some of the reviews she'd written but had added a bit of snark to make them more entertaining for her readers?

She thought about the syndication deal. She'd landed it based on her work with *Big Apple Weekly*, but she wasn't so sure it was what she wanted to do anymore. She should be proud of her work, but she wasn't proud of some of the things she'd done.

Her mother was right. She needed to get back to New York. She had some hard decisions to make. It was time to see them through.

Chapter 19

Torrian swept into his sister's office at the Fire Starter Grille. Theo leaned against the wall with his arms crossed over his mammoth-sized chest. Deirdre sat behind her desk. The tension in the office was thick as chimney smoke.

"Good, you're both here," Torrian said.

"You asked me to come," Theo said.

"I didn't know if you would," Torrian answered.

"You've been the one ignoring me, Wood, not the other way around."

"I know. I'm sorry, man. I just needed to get some things straight in my head."

"And you have?" Deirdre asked.

"Almost," Torrian answered. "I'm getting there. The meeting I just had with Sabers' management just took me one giant step forward." He couldn't wipe the huge grin from his face. "They offered me a coaching position."

"What?" Deirdre and Theo both barked.

Torrian nodded. "Avery Collins just accepted the head coaching position in Cincinnati. They moved Josh Newton to offensive coordinator, leaving a vacancy at wide receivers coach. My eyes may not be good enough for the field, but I can coach."

"Oh my God, Torrian." Deirdre ran from behind her desk and enveloped him in a hug. "I'm so happy for you."

"Congratulations, Dawg," Theo said, clapping Torrian on the back and pulling him in for a one-arm hug.

"Thanks, man. Guess you'll be seeing me a bit more these days, huh."

"Not unless you're up in the press box," Theo answered.

"You took the job?"

Theo nodded, a grin spreading across his face.

"What job?" Deirdre asked.

"I'm retiring from football after the season is over," Theo told her.

"Yeah, my man got an offer for this cushy commentator job."

"You're quitting?" Deirdre asked.

"Not quitting, retiring," he answered. "There's a difference."

"I didn't mean to imply…"

"Forget it," Theo cut her off.

Torrian glared at Theo. "Hey, Dee, you think I can get a reservation for lunch? Theo and I need to celebrate."

"Of course." She gave him another kiss on the cheek. "Congratulations again, honey." She turned to Theo. "Good luck with your new job."

"Thanks," he answered with as much emotion as a lump of coal.

Torrian refrained from speaking until they were seated at one of only a few tables available in the restaurant. "What's going on with you and my sister?" Torrian started.

"Not a damn thing," Theo answered.

"You sure? Because I think I saw a bit of hurt in Dee's eyes, and I told you what would happen if you hurt my sister."

"Your sister didn't give me a chance, okay. She shot down every attempt I made at getting to know her better. And after asking her out for the fifth time, she straight up told me she didn't want anything to do with me." Theo shrugged. "I'm just granting her wish."

"What's her wish? For you to act like an ass?"

"Are we going to celebrate our new jobs or debate who's being the bigger ass when it comes to the women in our lives?"

"Hey, man, don't try to put me in your league."

"Really?" Theo deadpanned. "Do you *want* me to bring her up?"

Torrian clenched his jaw. "You win."

Theo's cell phone rang. He pulled it from his pocket and held up a finger. "It's Latoya. I forgot I was supposed to meet her for lunch today."

While Theo talked to his sister, Torrian signaled the waiter for more wine.

"Oh damn," Theo muttered. He dragged a hand down his face. "When did you find out? No, I'm…uh, I'm with him right now. I'll tell him."

They were talking about him? An uneasy feeling settled in Torrian's stomach. He rapped his fist on the table, trying to catch Theo's attention.

"Yeah, Toya, I know you didn't mean for this to happen," Theo said. "I'll talk to you later." He ended the call and tossed the phone on the table with an aggravated grunt.

"What in the hell is going on? Did Latoya see something on my latest test?"

Theo shook his head. "She would never share medical info with me." He sighed. "Toya forgot her cell phone in the office.

When she went back for it, she found Paul Mixon, the pediatric ophthalmologist who shares her practice, rifling through her files. She confronted him and eventually got Mixon to admit he was the one who leaked your eye condition to the press."

Shock rooted Torrian to his seat. In the blink of an eye he saw the scenario play out in his head like a movie: Mixon stumbling over his record, the surprise on his face at finding the disease Torrian had tried to hide for so long, the call to Barry Stein, the one reporter who would relish unleashing such pain upon Torrian.

There was one person missing from the picture.

Paige.

"Oh God." Torrian cradled his head in his hands.

"I'm sorry, Wood," Theo offered.

"I accused her," Torrian whispered to himself. Shaking his head from side to side, his mind bombarded him with images of Paige from the last time he'd seen her. The hurt on her face. No, not hurt. There had been *pain*. She'd flinched at every horrible word he'd hurled at her.

He'd wanted to hurt her that night. He'd wanted to inflict some of the agony he'd been feeling from her betrayal.

But she hadn't betrayed him.

"What have I done?" Torrian said. He looked up at Theo. "I blamed Paige for all of this. If you only knew some of the things I said to her. God, Theo, I hurt her so much."

"You didn't know, Wood."

"You think that matters?" he asked loud enough to cause the heads from several tables around them to turn.

"Hey, c'mon, let's take this to Deirdre's office."

"No," Torrian said, pushing back from the table. "I need to find her."

"Now?" Theo asked.

"Yesterday," Torrian answered.

* * *

Torrian signed the visitor's log and followed the security guard's directions to the bank of elevators. He knew he was taking a chance, visiting her at work. But when he didn't find her at her apartment earlier he'd had no choice. He had to see her.

As he rode to the eighth floor where *Big Apple Weekly*'s offices were housed, he imagined how the next ten minutes would play out.

He would grovel. Torrian knew that with certainty. It was nothing less than he deserved. After everything he'd accused Paige of doing, groveling was the least he could do on the road to earning back the trust he knew he'd lost.

God, he'd missed her these last few weeks.

As much as he'd tried to push her out of his heart, not a second went by that he didn't think about her and the time they'd shared. It had been torture to remember those weeks they'd spent together, because thoughts of her betrayal were never far behind. But it had been a torture Torrian had come to embrace, because nothing hurt more than not thinking of Paige at all.

He exited the elevator and stepped through the frosted glass doors of *Big Apple Weekly*.

"Welcome to Big Apple…hey." The receptionist's eyes lit up. "You're—"

"Torrian Smallwood. Yes. Is Paige Turner here?"

"She's—"

"No," another woman said from within the office across from the reception desk. She stopped at the door, crossed her arms over her chest and leaned against the doorjamb.

"Do you know where she is?" Torrian asked.

"Paige doesn't work here anymore," she answered. "She quit about three weeks ago."

"Did she already start the job with the Cambridge Group?"

"No. She turned down the syndication deal."

"She *what?*"

"I guess you haven't noticed that her column hasn't appeared anywhere for weeks."

Torrian shook his head. He'd purposely avoided any newspaper or magazine that may have carried her syndicated column. He couldn't stomach seeing the byline he thought she'd sold him out to obtain.

"That deal was everything she's worked so hard for. Why would she turn it down?"

"I really don't know, because you're right, she has worked hard her entire career to get to this point. And just like that, she turned her back on it."

The thought that he had something to do with Paige's decision caused a sick feeling to churn in Torrian's gut.

"Where is she?" he asked.

"If Paige wanted you to know she would have contacted you."

"Angela," the receptionist interrupted. "You have a call."

"I have to go," the woman said before stepping back into her office and shutting the door.

For several moments Torrian stared at her through the glass window, but she never gave him a second glance. Paige had talked about Angela often, but he'd never met her. Now Torrian knew why the woman had been so cold. Angela and Paige were more than just colleagues; they were good friends.

Torrian turned to the receptionist. "Do you have any idea where Paige is?"

She shook her head, an apologetic expression on her face. "She didn't say when she left the magazine. Angela is probably the only one she's still in contact with from the office."

He wasn't getting anything out of Angela.

Forty minutes later, he was at his desk firing up his computer. He typed in *Paige Turner* into the search engine.

It generated thousands of results. There were links to her blog, archived articles she'd written, and Webcasts of their cooking segments from *Playing with Fire*. Torrian sat at the computer for a solid hour. He tried every combination of words he could think of to find her.

Just as he was about to throw caution to the wind and try her on her cell, a link caught his eye. It was dated two days ago. He clicked on the link. It took him to the home page of the *Harlem Sentinel*.

The Web site touted itself as a virtual soldier in the fight to reveal the positive side of Harlem. There were articles about various community activities, a neighborhood hero spotlight and a calendar of events. At the very bottom of the home page was the information Torrian had been hoping to find.

It read: "*The Harlem Sentinel* welcomes our newest associate editor, Paige Turner."

"Thank God," Torrian said with a deep sigh. He'd found her. He wrote down the address on a scrap of paper and punched it into his GPS system once he slid behind the wheel of his car.

It took over an hour to drive the eight miles to Harlem. He turned from Fredrick Douglass Boulevard onto West 136th Street, moving slowly as he checked building numbers. He pulled up to a brownstone that wasn't all that different from his own. A car was pulling from the curb, and he quickly parallel parked into the space.

Anticipation rushed through his blood. He knew he'd missed her, but until this moment, when he was mere minutes from seeing her face again, Torrian hadn't realized just how much his mind, body and soul craved this woman. He needed her like he needed air. It's why his world had been suffocating without her.

He rushed up the steps and tried the handle, but it was locked. The buzzer panel next to the door indicated there were four offices in the building. Just as he was about to buzz *The Harlem Sentinel*, the front door opened, and Paige emerged from the building.

She stared at him, not saying a word.

He stared back, doing likewise. She was so beautiful that she robbed the breath from his lungs.

After several moments, Paige asked, "What are you doing here?"

"I...I needed to see you," Torrian managed.

"Why?" she asked, moving past him and heading for the sidewalk. "Want to serve me with papers for a slander lawsuit?"

Torrian followed her down the stairs. "Paige, I know you weren't the one who told Stein," he called.

She stopped, turned.

He stared into her eyes and almost lost himself in their beauty. God, he'd missed her so much he ached from it.

"I'm sorry," he said. It's what he should have said from the very beginning.

Ignoring his apology, she said, "I already know I wasn't the one who told Stein." She folded her arms across her chest. "When did you figure it out?"

"Another doctor in Latoya's practice confessed to leaking my condition to the press."

She nodded, turned and started walking away from him without a word.

Torrian reached for her arm, "Paige, wait!"

She whipped around and grilled him with her glare. "You know, Torrian, for a second there I thought maybe you had just a little bit of faith in me. But now I realize if that doctor hadn't come clean, you would have gone the rest of your life thinking I'd stabbed you in the back. Sell your apology to someone else, because I'm not buying it."

"Paige, please," Torrian pleaded, wishing to God he'd never accused her. After everything they had been through, for him to have cast her to the wolves without ever listening to her side of the story was the most faithless thing he could have done. She was giving him exactly what he deserved.

"Try to see it from my perspective," he said. "The only people who knew about my eye condition were me, Theo, Latoya and you. Theo and Latoya had never said anything in all the time they'd known. Then the story breaks days after I shared my condition with you. What else was I supposed to think?"

"That I respected your privacy enough never to share something you'd told me in confidence. What you were *not* supposed to think is that I was selfish and ruthless enough to end your career just to further my own."

She pierced him with a look that shot straight to his heart. "You have no idea how much you hurt me. I'd fallen in love with you, and you tossed me away as if I were a piece of trash."

Torrian shut his eyes, unable to stomach the sight of the pain he'd caused her. An even more frightening realization gripped his gut—the fear that he'd lost her forever. He couldn't let that happen.

"Forgive me," Torrian said softly. "I would do anything to make this up to you, if you only give me a chance."

"Why should I?" she asked. "Would you have forgiven me if the doctor hadn't come clean? Answer me," she said. "Why should I forgive you, Torrian?"

"Because I love you," Torrian answered. "More than anything I've ever loved before, and anything I'll ever love again. Please, Paige, give me another chance."

Torrian's heart thumped a wild beat in his chest as he waited for her response, then shattered into a million pieces when she turned and walked away.

Chapter 20

Paige sat on a bench, watching as park goers moved along with their day. She didn't want to go back to her apartment. Although she should probably spend as much time there as possible, seeing as she would have to give it up soon. Her pay at the *Sentinel* was half of what she'd made at *Big Apple Weekly*. And the lack of free meals from restaurants she had to review was seriously cutting into her food budget.

But Paige had no desire to sit on her big green chair and stare at the space between those four walls. There were too many fresh memories there. During those weeks she'd wanted to keep their—whatever it is they'd had together—secret, she and Torrian had spent most of their time at her place. Now, Paige couldn't stomach being there alone.

"Suck it up, Olivia," she said under her breath.

She pushed herself up from the bench. She was not going to hide from her life just because Torrian had swept in, turned it upside down and swept back out again.

But he'd come back.

As she headed out of the park, her mind replayed the scene that had unfolded on the sidewalk in front of the *Sentinel*. She'd been too shocked at seeing Torrian to fully comprehend the first thing out of his mouth, but she'd heard him say that it was another doctor who'd leaked his medical information to the press. And she'd heard his apology loud and clear.

Then threw it right back in his face.

Paige mulled over the rest of what he'd said. As she thought it over with a more open mind, she could see how the process of elimination would leave her as the likeliest suspect. Why wouldn't he think it was her? He knew about her ambition to be a high-profile reporter. What would be more high-profile than helping to break the sports scandal of the year?

Paige thought about some of the other things she'd done to further her career, like writing reviews geared more toward what she knew her readers would want instead of what she'd truly felt in her heart. She'd compromised the value she held most dear—honesty. How could she blame Torrian for thinking anything different of her?

He had every right to point the finger at you.

Yet as soon as he discovered he'd been wrong he'd come straight to her. And she'd had the audacity to throw his apology in his face.

"Paige, you fool," she said, picking up the pace as she made her way through the park. He had come back to her, and she'd pushed him away. She would not let him get away again.

She loved him.

Urgency pulsed through Paige's blood like a rushing river. She had to find Torrian. He would likely be at the restaurant. After a quick stop at her place, she would go to the Fire Starter Grille and beg for his forgiveness if she had to. It would be the very least she could do after the way she'd treated him today.

Paige came upon her building and stopped short.

Torrian was sitting on the top step, elbows on his knees, his gloved hands clasped.

For long moments they simply stared at each other. Paige climbed the first step, and Torrian stood. She took the second step, and he stepped down to the third and held his hand out so she could join him.

"You can tell me to go, but I couldn't leave things the way they were," he said.

"I'm not going to tell you to go, Torrian. I wouldn't let you get away if you tried."

Understanding crept into his eyes, lighting them as her words sunk in.

"I'm sorry for the things I said to you," Paige continued.

"You don't have to apologize."

"Oh, I do," she said.

"I should have trusted you."

"No, you shouldn't have," Paige said. "Not too long ago, I would have done exactly what you accused me of doing. That's just how much getting ahead meant to me." She took his hands and brought them up to her lips, kissing the soft leather of his gloves. "But I found something that means even more to me. And I don't want to lose him. Ever."

He grabbed her by the neck and crushed her to him. "Oh God, Paige," he breathed into her ear. He pulled her away just enough to rest his forehead on hers.

"I love you so much," he said. The moisture of his breath tickled her face; the fierceness of his words warmed her soul.

"I love you, too, Torrian. Please say that you'll forgive me."

"There's only one thing I'll never forgive you for," he said. Paige looked up and stared into his eyes. "Leaving me again," he finished.

A grin spread across her lips. "You'll never have to worry about that," she assured him. "I'm here to stay."

* * * * *

L♥VE IN THE LIMELIGHT

Fantasy, Fame and Fortune...Hollywood-Style!

Book #1
By *New York Times* and *USA TODAY*
Bestselling Author Brenda Jackson

STAR OF HIS HEART
August 2010

Book #2
By A.C. Arthur

SING YOUR PLEASURE
September 2010

Book #3
By Ann Christopher

SEDUCED ON THE RED CARPET
October 2010

Book #4
By *Essence* Bestselling Author Adrianne Byrd

LOVERS PREMIERE
November 2010

*Set in Hollywood's entertainment industry,
two unstoppable sisters and their two friends
find romance, glamour and dreams-come-true.*

KIMANI
ROMANCE

www.kimanipress.com
www.myspace.com/kimanipress

REQUEST YOUR FREE BOOKS!

2 FREE NOVELS
PLUS 2 FREE GIFTS!

KIMANI™
ROMANCE

Love's ultimate destination!

Silhouette® Desire

New York Times and **USA TODAY**
bestselling author

BRENDA JACKSON

brings you

WHAT A WESTMORELAND WANTS,

another seductive Westmoreland tale.

Part of the Man of the Month series

Callum is hopeful that once he gets
Gemma Westmoreland on his native turf
he will wine and dine her with a seduction plan
he has been working on for years—one that
guarantees to make her his.

Available September wherever books are sold.

**Look for a new Man of the Month
by other top selling authors each month.**

Always Powerful, Passionate and Provocative.

SD73048